PENN

A CHARMIN
BUT WHAT S~~ECRETS LIE BENEATH?~~

Imagine...

A picturesque spa town and pretty villages that
nestle deep in the heart of England.

Pennington Country...

In Pennington the streets are filled with old-
fashioned buildings, attractive tearooms and
irresistible shops. In the surrounding villages of
Chastlecombe, Stavely and Swancote elegant manor
houses rub shoulders with cosy stone cottages, and
all the gardens are ablaze with flowers.

Pennington Lives...

And beneath the smooth surface the passions run
high – overwhelming attraction, jealousy, desire,
anger...and once-in-a-lifetime love.

Next month in Catherine George's
Pennington series:
NO MORE SECRETS

Catherine George was born in Wales, and early on developed a passion for reading which eventually fuelled her compulsion to write. Marriage to an engineer led to nine years in Brazil, but on his later travels the education of her son and daughter kept her in the UK. And instead of constant reading to pass her lonely evenings she began to write the first of her romantic novels. When not writing and reading she loves to cook, listen to opera, browse in antiques shops and walk the Labrador.

She has written over 60 romantic novels.

Praise for Catherine George:

'Catherine George...keeps readers thoroughly entranced.'
—*Romantic Times*

'Ms George has a captivating way of leaving her readers wanting more.'
—*theromancereadersconnection.com*

Summer of the Storm

by
Catherine George

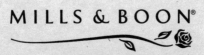

MILLS & BOON®

First published in Great Britain 1994. This edition 2003.
Harlequin Mills & Boon Limited,
Eton House, 18-24 Paradise Road, Richmond, Surrey, TW9 1SR

© Catherine George 1994

ISBN 0 263 83687 8

144-0703

Printed and bound in Spain
by Litografia Rosés S.A., Barcelona

Dear Reader

Following (humbly) the example of Thomas Hardy and his Casterbridge, I decided to create my own fictional town for the location of many of my novels. The result is the Cotswolds town of Pennington Spa, a place of thriving modern commerce located in classical buildings which, like its Pump Rooms, date from the Regency era, when drinking the waters was all the rage. Having lived in two attractive county towns in the past, I've taken features from both and added fictional ones of my own to invent a town of wide streets, leafy squares and crescents, with buildings in the local golden stone and public gardens bright with seasonal flowers. There are several hotels, numerous restaurants, parks, cinemas, a theatre and, of course, irresistible specialist shops which sell clothes, jewellery, contemporary furniture and fine art, alongside others which offer bargains to the antiques hunter.

To me, Pennington and its nearby towns and villages – Chastlecombe, Swancote, Stavely, Abbots Munden – are the dream combination of prosperity and timeless charm. I just wish Pennington really existed, so I could live there.

Best wishes

Catherine George

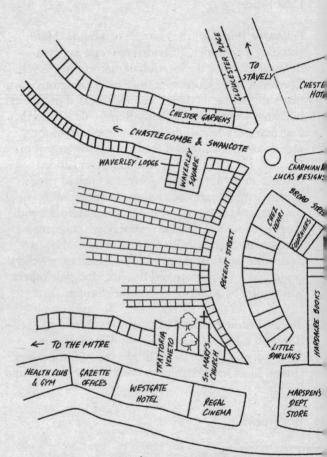

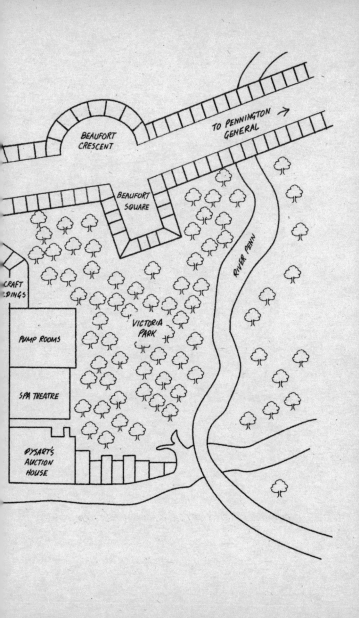

CHAPTER ONE

IF THE muted grey and pink décor was intended to soothe the occupants of the waiting-room, it was failing badly with one of them. Cassie fiddled with the bandage on her left hand, cold with dread at the thought of having the stitches out. She'd been brave enough when they went in, to a hand still numb after the operation. But today it was very much alive, and in a minute or two she'd have to tough it out and try not to make a complete fool of herself when the expert needlework was unpicked. To make matters worse, her carpal tunnel had been friendly Mr Parkinson's last operation before his retirement, which meant that today she was at the mercy of some stranger. She shivered, trying to concentrate on the glossy magazine on her lap, but each time a buzzer sounded her stomach gave a sickening lurch and she kept her eyes glued to the shaking pages, hoping it wasn't her turn. But all too soon it was.

'Miss Fletcher,' called the receptionist. 'Will you go in?'

Cassie smiled wanly, crossed the dove-grey carpet at a snail's pace, knocked on the consulting-room door and went in.

'Sit down, please,' called a voice from behind a screen.

Cassie sat, only vaguely aware of running water and scrubbing sounds. Her attention was centred on her hand, which had begun to throb and burn all along the incision. This is nonsense, she told herself irritably. You are an adult. You don't make a fuss over a few stitches. A couple of minutes and it will all be over.

She looked up with a resolute smile as a tall figure emerged from behind the screen. And in a flash all thoughts of her hand were wiped clean from Cassie's brain as she stared at the man seating himself behind the desk. He looked up with a polite smile which died the same death as hers. His piercing blue eyes narrowed in astonishment, fell to the notes in front of him, then returned to Cassie's frozen face.

There was a long pause while two stunned people gazed at each other in recognition.

'*Cassie*?' he said blankly, the clipped, husky voice as familiar to her now as the last time she'd heard it, more than ten years before. '*You're* Catherine Fletcher? I didn't make the connection.' He paused, his face suddenly expressionless. 'I always assumed your name was Cassandra.'

Cassie pulled herself together with effort. 'Alec Neville! What a surprise. Does this mean *you're* taking Mr Parkinson's place?'

'Is that so hard to believe?' Alec Neville held her eyes. 'You hadn't heard I've succeeded to his crown?'

'No.' She was in more command of herself by now. 'I knew Mr Parkinson was retiring, of course. In fact he only did the operation for me as a favour. Told me it was his swansong. I hadn't heard who was taking his place.'

'Then the grapevine at Pennington General must have changed a lot since my time!'

'I'm sure it's still in good working order. But it's years since I worked in the path lab there, Alec.' She paused, flushing slightly. 'Or perhaps you'd prefer Mr Neville now you've reached such exalted heights.'

He shrugged. 'You're paying. Call me what you like. Though I'm surprised you had the carpal tunnel done privately. Why didn't you save your money and have it done in Pennington General? It's a simple operation.'

'I needed it done at a specific time. Hence the favour by Mr Parkinson.'

'I see.' Alec Neville looked at her again, taking his time about it. Cassie willed herself to sit perfectly still under the scrutiny until he got to his feet. 'Come over to the couch, then, please,' he said briskly. 'I'll take a look at the hand.'

Cassie followed him across the room glumly to perch on the edge of the chair beside the couch, extending a shrinking arm to let him remove the bandages and dressing from her palm.

'You're very nervous,' he said quietly, his deft fingers gentle.

'Utterly terrified. I'm a coward,' she admitted

frankly, biting her lip at the sight of bruised, puffy flesh and the line of stitches along the short incision running from her wrist to the centre of her palm. She turned her head away sharply, trying not to wince as Alec Neville made a swift examination.

'We'll leave the stitches another week,' he said, applying a fresh dressing.

Cassie turned back in dismay. 'You mean I've got to come here again?'

His lips twitched as he fastened a clip in the bandage round her wrist. 'I'm afraid so.'

Cassie tried to smile as she got to her feet. 'Nothing personal, you understand. It was just that I'd braced myself to have the stitches out today, and now I'll have it hanging over me like a cloud all week again.'

Alec Neville raised an amused black eyebrow. 'You surprise me. The Cassie I once knew wouldn't have been afraid of anything.'

'I've changed a lot since those days.' She eyed him thoughtfully. 'So have you.'

'Only superficially,' he assured her. 'I get my hair cut short and earn more money, but otherwise I'm still the same old Alec Neville.'

Cassie nodded. 'I thought perhaps you might be.'

His eyes narrowed. 'Now what, I wonder, do you mean by that?'

'Nothing untoward.' Her smile was tinged with acidity. 'I suppose I meant I'm not surprised by your elevated status, Alec. All you ever talked about was making it to the top.' She extended her good hand. 'Thank you. It was nice to meet you again.'

'You'll be forced to again next week,' he reminded her drily.

Her face fell. 'Don't remind me.'

'I'm sorry the prospect's so daunting.'

'Only because you'll be unpicking my stitches!'

He released her hand, studying her face at length. 'You really have changed, Cassie. And not because it's ten years since I last saw you, either. You were so self-contained then, and now—'

'And now I'm making a terrible fuss about having a few stitches out.' She withdrew her hand firmly, and smiled. 'And I'm ten years older, too. Let's not forget that.'

'You don't look it, Cassie.'

'Why, thank you, kind sir!'

'It's the hair that's so different,' he commented, eyeing the unruly mane threatening to escape from the outsize tortoiseshell barrette keeping it in check at the nape of her neck. 'What have you done to it?'

'Nothing. I just let it do its own thing these days.' She looked away. 'I used to go to extraordinary lengths to straighten it when—when I worked in the path lab.'

Alec Neville looked at her in silence, seemed on the point of saying something further, then turned abruptly and went to the door to open it for her, very much the formal consultant again. 'Goodbye, then.

Ask the receptionist for a four-thirty appointment next Thursday.'

'Thank you—Mr Neville.' She gave him a polite smile, and left him to his next patient.

On her way home Cassie sat in the taxi in a state of shock, utterly shattered by the surprise of meeting with Alec again. Memories she'd thought forgotten came rushing back in spate at the mere sight of him, flooding the ten-year gap since he'd bidden her a furious goodbye and stormed out of her life. She smiled ruefully. It was hard to imagine the suave, polished consultant of today's session getting steamed up about anything. The new star of the Burns Unit was a far cry from the Alec Neville who'd turned Cassie Fletcher's life upside down all those years ago.

The day he'd burst into the path lab demanding instant results on tissue removed from one of his patients the young Cassie's first reaction had been hostility. His reputation had gone before him. She'd heard far too much about the charismatic registrar who had all the nurses in the hospital panting after him. And his physical appearance did him no favours as far as Cassie was concerned, either. In those days Alec had affected hair in corkscrew curls and a gold ring in one ear, and the dark fatigue marks under his weary blue eyes had given him more the look of a debauched rock star than a doctor, despite the white coat and stethoscope of his calling. For calling it was. Alec Neville's dedication to his profession was as legendary at the General as his love-affairs, which, like everything else in his life, came second to his job—something Cassie Fletcher had recognised all too clearly right from the beginning.

Cassie came to with a start as the taxi drew up outside her home. She fumbled in her bag with one hand for money to pay the driver, then lingered a little in the garden as the car drove away, promising the flowerbeds she'd weed them as soon as she had two hands in working order again. She looked up at the thatched roof and irregular windows of Combe Cottage with her usual surge of possessiveness, then went inside and locked the door on the world.

At some time in its past history Combe Cottage had been assisted very gently into the present by owners careful to preserve its personality. The result was harmonious. Two rooms had been knocked into one at the back of the house to make a kitchen large enough to allow room for eating as well as cooking. In the front portion there was a dining-room which Cassie used as an office, and a low-ceilinged sitting-room with an inglenook fireplace and exposed beams. The minuscule front hall gave straight on to stairs of ladder-like steepness, which led to one large bedroom, one smaller one and a bathroom. To Cassie, who'd spent some of her earlier life in a grim little terraced house in Pennington, the cottage in the village of Combe Aston was everything she'd ever dreamed of. Well, almost everything, she amended honestly, and went to change her dress for leggings and T-shirt.

With the dexterity she'd quickly developed since

the operation, she made herself a mug of coffee one-handed while she listened to the messages on her answering machine.

'Shan't inflict myself on you this Sunday, after all, Cass,' said a familiar, laughing voice. 'Heavy date. Hope your hand's all right. See you next week—maybe.'

Cassie chuckled, not sorry to be saved the bother of cooking an enormous meal with her present limitations. Her brother Ben was large, with an appetite to match.

'Liam here,' said the next voice on the machine. 'Cassie, I can't get away tonight. Hellish sorry—usual reason. See you Saturday?'

Heigh-ho, sighed Cassie, as she sat down with her coffee. Tonight would be quiet after all. It wasn't unusual for Detective Inspector Liam Riley of the Pennington CID to find his work in the way of his social life—and hers—but on occasion it was a bit maddening if she'd cooked a special meal or planned something specific in his company. Tonight, however, she was rather glad to be on her own. The meeting with Alec Neville had shaken her considerably. It had been a shock to come face to face with the man who'd broken her heart all those years ago. Not that her heart had remained in pieces. It had mended in time, as hearts did. After ten years, her main reaction to the sight of him, she assured herself, had been perfectly natural surprise.

Nevertheless, left with an evening to herself, Cassie

felt restless. With only one hand in use, her usual all-purpose therapy of gardening was out of the question. And the evening, though gloriously sunny, had an end-of-term feel about it. Summer was packing up to leave. There was a definite autumn nip in the air as Cassie wandered round the large garden at the back of the cottage. The blackberries on the boundary hedge were already ripe, she noticed glumly, and some of the leaves on the trees were already turning.

Not that the season had caused her mood, she knew perfectly well. The meeting with Alec was to blame. One look at him and the mature Cassie Fletcher, these days so well-balanced and comfortable with herself, had reverted to a girl of twenty at the mercy of her emotions.

She turned suddenly and went back into the house to rummage in the cupboard under the stairs for an old photograph album. Wiping the dust off the cover, she took it into the sitting-room and flipped through it until she found the pages which held the pictorial record of her romance with Alec Neville. For romance it had been, right enough. He'd swept into her life like a hurricane, transformed her life for the duration of one long, hot summer, then swept out again, leaving far too much emotional wreckage in his wake.

Cassie stared down at the inexpert series of snapshots. The sun had always seemed to shine when she was with Alec. She'd owned a second-hand camera and had taken as many shots of him as he'd allow: Alec, long, lanky and restless, squinting in the sun, with hands on his slim hips, his ridiculous ringlets falling in his eyes, and the gold ring glinting defiantly in his ear. There were other shots of Alec throwing a ball for Cassie's dog, posing theatrically with a smirk on his face, and lying, exhausted and vulnerable in sleep by a riverbank, worn out from the disturbed nights and cruelly long hours of his job at Pennington General.

The photographs he'd taken of Cassie showed a young, sober girl with hair pulled back in a tight braid, and a wary look in her dark eyes, as though she knew from the start it would all end in tears.

The rest of the pages were blank, as though nothing had been worth photographing after Alec's departure. Cassie banged the album shut with a sudden shiver and jumped to her feet to stare into the old Victorian mirror she'd bought herself for her birthday. When Alec Neville had left Pennington for London and the next rung of his ladder she'd felt as though her life was over. To start it up again she'd tried hard to make herself into someone different from the girl he'd known. She'd given up using the enormous rollers which straightened her hair. Tempted to have the unruly mass cut short, she had been influenced by sheer lack of funds into leaving her crowning glory to its own devices. She had skewered it up in a topknot for the path lab, buried herself in her work and doggedly done her best to forget that Alec Neville had ever existed.

Cassie shook her head at her reflection. So now she

was the one with the wild hair and Alec Neville wore his cut in some expensive clever way which tamed it to lie close to his head, with no sign of an earring now he was a sober consultant. He was heavier, too. Ten years ago he'd been just as tall, but with barely enough flesh to cover his bones. Nowadays Alec Neville's build was powerful, with muscles discernible even through the expensive cloth of his suit.

Cassie's oval eyes flashed suddenly, and she turned away from the mirror with an exclamation of disgust. Alec Neville's muscles were none of her business. Even if she still had any stupid hankerings for him— which she hadn't—by this time he was no doubt married to some influential medical man's daughter and probably had a family, a large house, several cars and a lifestyle so far removed from her own that after the appointment with him in a week's time their paths were unlikely to cross again.

Unable to work in the garden or in her office, Cassie was glad when Saturday came with the prospect of company for the day. But when Liam arrived he wasn't alone. With him, hanging on to each of his hands as they emerged from the car, were his twins, Kitty and Tess.

He smiled sheepishly as Cassie went down the path to greet them. Liam Riley was large and tough-looking, with a broken nose and blue eyes ringed with lashes as black as his hair. Allowing for certain differences his nine-year-old daughters were so like him it was comical.

'Well, hello, girls,' said Cassie, surprised, and shot a speaking look at Liam. 'I didn't know you two were coming.'

'Dett asked me to switch Saturdays at the last minute,' said Liam, eyeing her warily. 'Something about taking her mother to visit a sick friend.'

Detta Riley had divorced Liam over a year before, unable to come to terms with the exigencies of her husband's job, and, while it was she who laid down the law about Liam's reasonable access to his daughters, she also played ducks and drakes with the rules whenever it suited her. Which happened all too often when Liam arranged to spend time at Combe Cottage, or anywhere else, with Cassie Fletcher.

'You'll have to take us out somewhere to eat, then,' said Cassie, as they went into the house. She waved her hand at him. 'The stitches didn't come out after all.'

'Does it hurt, Cassie?' enquired Kitty with ghoulish interest. 'Can we see your stitches?'

'No, darling. I've got to keep the dressing on, but I'll ask the doctor if I can bring the stitches home afterwards to show you.'

'When will that be?' asked Liam, as his daughters accepted beakers of orange juice.

'Thursday.'

'Old Parkinson obviously thought the wound needed to knit more—Tess, Kitty, have a run in the garden, then we'll go into Pennington for burgers.'

The twins made off at once to climb their favourite

tree, leaving a rather pregnant silence behind them in the kitchen.

'You mind,' said Liam at last, his eyes on hers.

'A little,' said Cassie honestly, then smiled quickly. 'Not about the twins. You know I'm fond of them. I just mind not being consulted first.'

He smiled morosely. 'If I had you might have said no. And it's over a week since I've seen you.'

'Then now you're here we'll make the best of it.' Cassie went to the window to watch the twins trying to climb one of the apple trees. She turned to smile at their father. 'Good thing they're in dungarees.'

Liam's mouth twisted. '*Designer* dungarees, needless to say. Detta spends all the money I give her on their clothes.'

'Detta must make good money herself,' Cassie pointed out. 'She's a skilled physiotherapist—'

'With a private practice and works at home,' Liam finished bitterly, 'not to mention a mother installed in the stable flat. Fat chance a policeman with irregular hours has of ever getting custody of his children when their mother's arrangements are so perfect!'

'Is custody what you want?' asked Cassie quietly.

Liam stared moodily through the window at the children, who were playing tag now, their voices shrill on the still air. 'Pointless wanting what I can't have. What I *do* want is more time with them.'

'Have another go at Detta about it,' said Cassie practically. 'But for the moment I suggest you concentrate on enjoying your time with them today.'

Liam turned suddenly and pulled her into his arms. 'First, how about kissing a lonely policeman, Cassie Fletcher?'

Cassie let him kiss her, trying to relax in his arms, but, as always when the twins were around, she found it difficult, relieved when they came running in so she could pull away.

The programme for the day, instead of a long laze in the garden, with dinner later at a country pub, as Cassie had hoped, was lunch in a burger bar in Pennington followed by a session at a cinema show-ing a re-run of *Ghostbusters*. Afterwards they bought cakes at a bakery and went back to Combe Cottage for tea.

When the twins were rapt in front of the television afterwards Liam went into the kitchen with Cassie to help wash up.

'Why did Parkinson decide to leave the stitches in?' he asked, frowning. 'Anything wrong with the wound?'

'No. It just needs to heal more.' Cassie hung mugs on hooks, her back turned to Liam. 'It wasn't Mr Parkinson,' she added casually. 'I saw the man who's taken over from him.'

'I heard the post was up for grabs. Who won the prize?'

Cassie kept her face carefully neutral. 'A man by the name of Alec Neville. Oddly enough I used to know him, years ago. He did a spell at Pennington General when I worked in the path lab there—' She broke off as the phone rang and went to her office to answer it, returning to Liam almost at once in resignation. 'It's for you.'

He groaned, swearing as he shot off into the other room.

Minutes later Liam Riley was on his way out, promising faithfully to come back for his daughters in time to take them home.

'Don't be late, for pity's sake,' said Cassie, alarmed. 'I don't want Detta descending on me like the angel of wrath. Have you forgotten I can't drive with this hand?'

Liam swore again. 'I'll send someone to pick them up if I can't make it, Cassie. Goodbye, my darlings, Daddy's got to rush.'

Kitty and Tess clung to him, protesting, but once he'd torn himself away agreed eagerly enough when Cassie suggested they get some fresh air in the garden after an afternoon spent in the cinema. She ran about energetically, playing ball with them, but after a few hectic minutes missed a particularly wild throw from Kitty and fell awkwardly. She let out a screech of pain as she landed on her hands and knees, most of her weight on her bandaged palm. The children rushed to her in consternation, in their panic making matters worse as one of them grasped her left arm to help her up.

'It's all—right—girls,' Cassie gasped, as she struggled to her feet. Clenching her teeth on a rush of

nausea, she did her best to smile down into two hor-
rified little faces. 'I'm fine. Honestly!'

'Perhaps I can help,' said a voice behind her and
Cassie swung round in blank astonishment to find
Alec Neville surveying the little trio with a very odd
look on his face as the twins, suddenly shy, moved
closer to Cassie at the sight of the stranger, their blue
eyes wide under mops of windblown black curls.

'Hello,' he said at last, smiling at them. 'Don't
worry. I shan't hurt Mummy. I'm a doctor.'

'Oh, but I'm not—' began Cassie, but Alec interrupted impatiently.

'I'd better take a look at that hand. I saw you fall
on it.'

'If you must, Alec, but I'm not—'

'You *are* in pain, Cassie. Your face is green.'

Cassie abandoned explanations and hastily led the
way indoors. Gulping hard, she sent Tess and Kitty
into the sitting-room to watch television again, and
directed Alec to the kitchen sink.

'Feel nauseated?' he asked, as he dispensed with
the bandage and dressing.

Cassie nodded, speechless by this time as she
fought to keep her lunch.

He eyed the incision closely, but apart from a
bruise around it, already an alarming midnight-blue,
there was no actual damage to the wound. 'You'll do.
No real harm done. Do you have any spare dressings
and some antiseptic?'

She nodded again.

'Get them, then, and I'll put you back together.'

Knees shaking, Cassie climbed the steep stairs to the bathroom, utterly mystified by Alec Neville's sudden appearance in her garden. She groaned as she caught sight of herself in the mirror, and hastily removed some leaves from her hair. Not daring to spare time for the smear of mud down the front of her cotton sweater, she collected the dressings and hurried back downstairs to find Alec laughing with the girls at the antics of some cartoon character.

He sprang up as she appeared. 'Right, let's sort you out.'

Alec Neville's hands were sure and deft as he swabbed the wound and dressed it. Cassie, with time to look at him more closely, noted a network of fine lines at the corners of his eyes, but no sign of the dark rings of fatigue she remembered from the old days. His face looked tanned and healthy against his white shirt collar and Cambridge blue sweater, and his perfectly cut linen trousers, she noted wryly, were a far cry from the disreputable jeans of his leisure time when he was on the surgical staff at Pennington General.

'You're very quiet, Cassie,' he commented, the rasp in his voice very much in evidence as he gave her back her hand. 'Did I hurt you?'

'Not much. I was admiring your sartorial elegance.' She smiled. 'A bit different from the old days.'

'In common with several things,' he said, a wry twist to his lips. 'How old are the twins?'

'Nine. But—' Cassie sighed as the phone rang. 'Excuse me a moment, Alec.'

It was Liam, stressed and apologetic, asking Cassie if she could possibly organise a taxi and get the twins back to Pennington herself. 'There's a flap on here— I just can't spare a squad car to take them.'

Cassie sighed. 'All right, Liam. What time are they due back?'

'Seven,' he said, sounding guilty. 'I know it's short notice—blast, I've got to go. I'll ring you later.'

Normally Cassie could appreciate that a policeman's lot wasn't always happy, but she was quite out of patience with Liam Riley when she found the only taxi willing to come out as far as Combe Aston couldn't make it before eight. She thrust her good hand through her hair in frustration as she stared through the window, then her eyes lit up. Parked at her very gate was a long, dark red vehicle doing absolutely nothing.

She ran back to the kitchen, where Alec was scrubbing his hands. 'Could I ask a big, big favour, Alec?'

He tore off a length of kitchen paper in lieu of a towel, eyebrows raised. 'Ask away.'

'Are you by any chance driving back to Pennington now?'

'Why?'

'I need to get the twins home. I can't drive with this hand and there isn't a taxi to be had before eight.'

He gave her a narrowed, steely look. 'Home?'

'Yes,' said Cassie urgently. '*Their* home. Their

mother's expecting them,' she added, noting a well-remembered tightening of Alec Neville's jaw.

'You let me think they were yours, Cassie,' he said coldly.

'So what? They might well have been. Anyway, I tried to explain earlier but you wouldn't listen.'

His face softened slightly. 'I was too intent on seeing to that hand.' He leaned against the sink, arms crossed. 'I've learnt that they answer to Kitty and Tess, but I didn't think to enquire about the rest. Who *do* they belong to?'

'Their father's a friend of mine,' said Cassie, flushing a little at his quizzical look. 'He's divorced from their mother and the twins live with her, of course. She asked him to look after them today.'

'So why the hell isn't he doing so?'

'Because he's a detective inspector with Pennington CID and lives at the beck and call of his job, just like a doctor,' said Cassie tartly. 'Some crisis blew up after tea and he had to take off.'

'Couldn't their mother come to fetch them?'

'I've no intention of asking Detta Riley to do anything! Look, if it's too much trouble,' added Cassie irritably, 'please don't bother. I'll wait for a taxi.'

Alec moved away from the sink, taking his car keys from his pocket. 'Of course I'll take them. Where do they live?'

'Chester Gardens, not far from the Pump Rooms.'

He nodded. 'Right. Go and clean yourself up, then, and we'll be off.'

Cassie bit her lip. '*Must* I come too?'

Alec eyed her sardonically. 'My dear girl, I don't relish driving up to some strange woman's house with her children in my car. Presumably she knows you?'

'Oh, yes, she knows me,' said Cassie acidly. 'By sight, at least. But you're right, of course. Give me five minutes.' She hurried off to collect the twins. 'Come on, girls, let's tidy up. Daddy can't get back in time for you so Mr Neville's taking you home in his car. I'm coming too,' she added reassuringly.

'Is it a nice car?' asked Kitty as Cassie shepherded them upstairs for a wash.

'Very nice indeed.'

'Goody,' said Tess, scrubbing at her face with a flannel. 'Mummy must be home from shopping by now.'

Cassie stiffened. '*Shopping*?'

Kitty nodded artlessly. 'She's gone to buy clothes with Granny. That's why she rang Daddy to fetch us. We don't like shopping much.'

I don't like Detta Riley much, either, thought Cassie vengefully, and ripped off her muddy sweater and leggings to change into a cream cotton knit dress she could manage with one hand. She threw a gold chain over her head, brushed out her hair, slid her bare brown feet into flat sandals, added a few swift touches to her face then inspected the twins to make sure they were presentable. When she led the way downstairs to the sitting-room she found Alec Neville lounging at ease on her sofa watching a newscast.

He sprang to his feet, his eyes narrowing a little at the sight of her, then held out his hands to the twins. 'Right then, ladies, your carriage awaits.'

The 'carriage' was a damson-red Daimler. Cassie whistled, impressed. 'Goodness, how grand!'

'The trappings of success,' he said dismissively, and busied himself with strapping in the twins at the back before removing a briefcase from the front seat so Cassie could get in. 'Can you manage your seatbelt with that hand?'

'Yes,' she assured him, suddenly mindful of her manners as he started the car. 'I'm very grateful, Alec. It's good of you to do this.'

He shrugged. 'No great thing. It's not far to Pennington.'

Cassie eyed him curiously as the car glided up the narrow lane to the main road. 'Which reminds me, what on earth brought you to Combe Aston this evening?'

'Reconnaissance.' He indicated the sheaf of papers protruding from the briefcase on the floor beside her. 'I'm house-hunting. Thought I'd explore a few areas before actually looking at properties. There were three in this neck of the woods—one right at the bottom of your lane, as it happens.'

Cassie blinked, strongly averse to the idea of Alec Neville living in such proximity. 'You won't like Marsh House,' she said emphatically. 'It's falling to bits.'

He slanted an amused look at her. 'You obviously don't relish the thought of me as a neighbour.'

She flushed, unable to deny it as Alec sent the big car purring along the main dual carriageway into the town.

'You looked thunderstruck when I turned up in your garden,' he said after a while.

'Absolutely. For a moment I couldn't believe my eyes.'

'I felt much the same.' Alec gestured towards the back seat.

Cassie giggled. 'You thought they were mine.'

'A not unnatural assumption.' He shrugged. 'I remembered your address from your notes. I was driving up the lane from Marsh House—which is a dump, just as you say—so when I saw you running about in the garden I stopped the car to say hello, just in time to see you keel over.'

'There's our house!' called Kitty, as they reached Chester Gardens.

Cassie glanced quickly at her watch.

'What's the matter?' demanded Alec. 'Are we late?'

'No, praise be—still three minutes to countdown.'

'Are you *afraid* of this woman, Cassie?' he asked softly, mindful of the ears in the back.

'Not for myself,' she whispered. 'For their father. He's the one who'd suffer.'

'Ah, yes, their father,' repeated Alec tonelessly,

then raised his voice as he brought the car to a halt. 'Here we are, ladies, safe and sound.'

As he got out to unfasten their seatbelts Kitty and Tess beamed up at Alec, thanking him in unison.

'My pleasure.' He bowed formally and helped them out. 'Hurry up, Cassie,' he added in an undertone.

To Cassie's relief Detta's mother answered the door, and the twins threw themselves on their grandmother, chattering like magpies about their day. Cassie interrupted to explain the reason for Liam's absence, bade a hasty goodbye to the twins and managed to regain the safety of the car before their mother could put in an appearance.

Probably putting her feet up, worn out with all that shopping, thought Cassie nastily, as she struggled with her seatbelt.

'Let me,' said Alec, and leaned across to fasten it, raising a caustic eyebrow at her instinctive recoil. 'Don't worry, Cassie, I don't bite.'

She coloured to the roots of her hair, then groaned as she saw Detta Riley appear in the doorway. 'Can we *go*, please?'

Alec's lips twitched as he turned the key in the ignition. 'I take it the militant-looking redhead is Mrs Riley. That's a baleful stare she's beaming in this direction, Cassie. Is it possible she's jealous of you?'

'No idea,' said Cassie irritably, and only relaxed when Chester Gardens was safely behind them and they were on the road to Combe Aston. An embarrassing run-in with Detta Riley was the last thing she'd fancied. 'I'm sorry you have to drive me back as well,' she said after a while.

'You needn't be. I've nothing planned for this evening, Cassie.'

Feeling ill at ease now she was alone with Alec in the car, Cassie made a determined effort at light conversation for a while, until he gave her a sidelong smile which told her he knew only too well what she was about.

'Relax, Cassie. You're nearly home now.' He turned his eyes to the road again. 'As a matter of interest, does the good inspector hold the monopoly on all your social time these days?'

Cassie frowned. 'No,' she said slowly, 'not exactly.'

'Then perhaps you might have dinner with me some time.'

She stared at his profile in astonishment. 'Why?' she asked baldly.

He gave her a sardonic look before returning his eyes to the road. 'Is that your usual response to dinner invitations, or only to mine?' He was quiet for a moment. 'To be honest, Cassie, it's not just your company I want. You owe me some explanation of what happened ten years ago. Meeting you again has revived my curiosity about what—or who—made you break up with me so suddenly. I vote we discuss it over a meal.'

'I don't feel I owe you anything,' Cassie retorted, then bit her lip, annoyed with herself. 'Besides,' she added more temperately, 'our situations are very different now.'

'By which I assume you mean your man would object,' said Alec swiftly.

Cassie shrugged. 'I wouldn't describe Liam as "my man" exactly, but I suppose I'd be a bit miffed if he *didn't* object.'

He gave her a satirical look. 'My interest lies solely in your reactions to the idea, not his.'

'You haven't said whether *you* have anyone who'd object,' Cassie pointed out.

'I don't. Not any more,' he added, in a tone which ruled out further questions. He stopped the car at her gate and turned in his seat to look at her. 'From the lack of enthusiasm I gather the idea doesn't appeal.'

He was wrong. The idea appealed so much that Cassie began to fumble with her seatbelt to hide the fact from the searching blue eyes trained on her face.

'Allow me.' Once again Alec leaned across her to release the catch, and Cassie sat motionless, her pulse racing as she breathed in the scent of his warm, fastidiously clean body, transported back without warning to the time when she'd been so helplessly, hopelessly in love with him.

Alec straightened, his face suddenly mask-like as he stared through the windscreen. 'After all this time I expected to find you married—if I found you at all.'

Did that mean he'd intended looking for her?

'I was on the point of marrying, once,' she admitted.

'What happened?'

'It didn't work out.'

'You mean you sent him packing—an old habit of yours.'

Cassie breathed in sharply. 'Alec, don't.'

'I can't believe you've had only one proposal. You've matured into a beautiful woman,' he went on smoothly, 'and you're a lot more at ease with yourself these days. When you were sweet and twenty you kept a tight rein on your natural instincts—except on one unforgettable occasion, of course.'

Cassie's head flew up, her eyes glittering angrily. 'That subject's taboo, Alec.'

Alec's eyebrows rose mockingly. 'Then you haven't forgotten. Very well, I'll respect your sensibilities on that particular topic, but Cassie, after all these years surely I deserve an explanation! Why *did* you send me away so suddenly?'

'I had my reasons,' she said doggedly.

'And wouldn't tell me what they were,' he said grimly. 'What a mystery lady you were, to be sure. Even when we arranged to meet you'd often as not cancel at the last minute. And you got in a terrible panic when I suggested meeting your family.' His mouth twisted. 'I even considered getting my hair cut at one time, convinced my appearance was the stumbling-block.'

Cassie laughed involuntarily. 'I don't believe you, Alec! Your earring and that outrageous hair were the gauntlets you flung down against conformity.'

'You remember that?' he said in surprise.

'You told me so often enough!'

He smiled wryly, then sobered. 'When I saw the twins with you I had quite a shock, Cassie.'

'Why? They could easily have been mine.'

'But you were still Cassie Fletcher, so I assumed you were still—'

'Available?' she suggested sweetly.

'When were you ever that? Unattached was the word I had in mind.' They exchanged a long level look, then Cassie smiled politely.

'Time I went in. I really mustn't keep you any longer.'

Alec leapt from the car swiftly and came round to help her out. 'So *will* you dine with me?'

Cassie withdrew her hand gently, her eyes steady on his as she summoned up the strength to refuse. 'No, Alec, it's wiser if I don't.'

'Wiser?' He smiled a little, his narrowed eyes holding hers.

Her chin went up. 'No point in upsetting Liam.'

'I see. Surely he couldn't object if you just ask me in for coffee?'

'Probably not, but I'm not going to.'

He looked down at her in sardonic enquiry, as though he knew the answer in advance. 'Why not?'

Cassie met the hard blue eyes very squarely. 'Because ''coffee'' is usually a euphemism for something quite different.'

'My dear Cassie,' drawled Alec, 'my sole aim was

a little more conversation with an old friend to bridge the years, not to rip your clothes off the minute we were through the door.'

'Then you really have changed, Alec!' she snapped back, annoyed.

He gave a short, unamused laugh. 'In actual fact I haven't much. I was no more a sex-mad animal ten years ago than I am now. Goodnight, Cassie.' And without another word he turned on his heel and strode down the path to the car.

CHAPTER TWO

CASSIE found it impossible to sleep that night, deeply disturbed by the fact that feelings she'd been so sure were dead and buried had resurrected themselves in full working order after a second meeting with Alec Neville. The first encounter in his consulting-room had been different. Then they'd been doctor and patient, despite the past. Tonight had been different. Tonight she'd been physically very much aware of him, and unless she was very much mistaken his reaction to her had been similar. She tossed and turned, trying to blot out the past, but it was no use. That summer ten years before kept running through her mind like an endless videotape which she managed to check before it reached the end, only to find it beginning all over again.

She'd been so determined not to fall in love with Alec Neville at first, mainly because so many other females at the General had succumbed to his charms before her, and gone round lamenting the fact afterwards when he went on to pastures new. And Alec Neville was renowned for his honesty about his intentions. He made it clear to all concerned that he was out for fun and games and a good time, with no strings and no tears when the brief flings were over.

Then Alec had met Cassie Fletcher, and from the first it was a very different story. Previously the others had done the falling in love. This time the feeling was mutual, and intense from the start, quite unlike anything that had happened to either of them before.

Cassie flopped over on her back and stared through the window at the stars, surrendering to the flood of memories she'd kept locked away for so long. Anything permanent had never been at all possible for them. She'd known that from the start. Alexander Murray Neville's family home was an Elizabethan manor house in the West Country. He was a product of Eton and Cambridge, already tipped for the top in his profession, with all the self-assured confidence such a background engendered. His brother was a surgeon, his elderly father a professor of medicine, his mother a tireless worker for charity in their community. And Alec Neville was still climbing the ladder towards success, with no intention of saddling himself with a wife and responsibility until he was much nearer the top.

He was honest to the point of bluntness about this to Cassie from the outset. And Cassie, whose home was a small, poky house in a terrace on the wrong side of Pennington, decided the chasm between his background and hers was too wide to attempt to bridge, and accepted the terms of their relationship without question, keeping him separate from her private life for a variety of reasons she had no intention of disclosing to Alec Neville or anyone else.

How stupid she'd been! Cassie, with the wisdom of ten years on, knew she should have been more open with Alec, let him judge for himself. But at the time she'd been desperate to prevent any intrusion on their idyll. And now he was back. Not back in her life necessarily, but very much back in Pennington, and the mere thought of having him within a ten-mile radius was more disturbing than she'd have believed possible.

In the cold light of day, tired and irritable and very much out of sorts, Cassie got up determined to put Alec Neville out of her head. To achieve it she tried her hand at some typing, eager to get back to work, but the hand protested and the dressing got in the way. Forced to give up, she made copious notes instead, caught up on a lot of research, did a little awkward, one-handed pruning in the autumn sunshine, talked to her mother on the telephone a lot and gave Liam such a warm welcome the one night that week he was free that he misunderstood her enthusiasm entirely and for the first time tried to rush her to bed. The result was an acrimonious argument which sent Liam storming off without eating the meal she'd taken such pains to prepare.

Cassie, shaken and angry, slammed the lid on the casserole, threw the baked potatoes in the bin, and stored the salad in a plastic box in the refrigerator. Afterwards she slumped in front of the television, watching an ancient black and white film with a pot of coffee for company while she consumed the entire contents of the large box of chocolates Liam had brought her. Not surprisingly, the pastime resulted in such an overdose of caffeine that Cassie's hand shook when she changed channels to watch the news.

Why couldn't she have let Liam make love to her? she asked herself irritably. Would it have been such a big deal? Then suddenly she sat very still, her heart giving an errant thump as the truth confronted her with a cold, basilisk stare. Liam Riley was an attractive, intelligent man and she was grateful to him for all the help he'd given her. But, however much she valued him as a friend, it was impossible to think of him as a lover now Alec Neville had materialised in her life again.

Next morning Cassie woke with such a blinding headache after the mammoth chocolate consumption that she wasn't nervous in the least when the taxi came to take her to St John's Nursing Home that afternoon. Until the day before she'd dreaded another meeting with Alec almost as much as having the stitches out. But now, as she winced in the taxi at every bump in the road, the pain in her head monopolised all her attention. It had even been too much trouble to smarten herself up. Her original intention had been to wear something elegant and morale-boosting, but in the end she'd gone as she was, in a navy T-shirt and navy-dotted white cotton trousers, with no vestige of make-up and her hair wilder than usual because she couldn't bear to brush it properly.

She got out of the car at Outpatients, her red-rimmed eyes shielded from the afternoon sunlight by large dark glasses as she paid the driver.

When Cassie was sent in to him Alec rose from behind his desk, eyebrows raised. 'Hello, Cassie—sit down, please. What's wrong? You look ill. Have you hurt your hand again?'

She shook her head rashly, and let out a little moan. 'Migraine,' she whispered, letting herself down in the chair gingerly.

'Or do you mean hangover?' he asked, eyeing her closely.

'Only from a chocolate binge.'

'Ah. I remember. You're still an addict, then.'

'Not any more. As from today I'm cured,' she said bitterly, and looked at him in stark appeal. 'Could we get on with it, *please*? I long to get home to a dark-ened room.'

'By all means. Come over to the couch.'

Cassie took off the sunglasses and laid them on the desk, then followed Alec across the room to sit in the chair he drew forward. She turned her head away as he removed the dressing and examined the wound.

'Very nice,' he said briskly, and Cassie tensed as she heard the clink of instruments.

'Could I have the stitches, please?' she asked, feel-ing foolish.

'Mementoes?'

'In a way.'

She clenched her teeth as he snipped, holding herself so rigid that the pain in her head grew intense enough to eclipse the fleeting burning sensations in her hand as Alec worked.

'All over,' he said, so quietly that she barely heard him before the room went dark and a peremptory hand pushed her much tried head between her knees.

After a moment or two Alec helped her sit up and led her to the bathroom door, which Cassie barely managed to close behind her before she was violently sick.

It was a long time before she could bring herself to leave her temporary sanctuary. When she did Alec was at his desk, writing up her notes. He waved her to the chair in front of him, eyeing her greenish pallor with professional interest.

'How do you feel?'

Cassie, feeling hideously embarrassed, replaced the sunglasses with a shaking hand. 'Like death,' she said faintly.

'Let me see your hand, please.' Alec studied the outstretched palm and nodded approvingly. 'It should heal rapidly now the stitches are out. Flex your fingers for me? Good. How does it feel?'

'Fine.'

'Right. Don't hesitate to get in touch if you're worried about it, but I don't anticipate problems. Tom Parkinson did a very neat job.' Alec stood up in dismissal. 'When you get home, take something for that head.'

'I will. Thank you. Could I have my stitches, please?'

He smiled indulgently, and held out a tissue-wrapped package. 'All six of them, neatly preserved. Goodbye, Cassie.' He held out his hand and she put her good one into it for a moment, then went through the door he held open for her, aching head held high.

Cassie, desperate to escape from St John's Nursing Home instantly and forever, listened in dismay when the receptionist reported that it would be at least half an hour before a taxi could come to pick Miss Fletcher up. Cursing herself for not asking Ben to drive her in, Cassie decided to walk to the main road and wait for a bus, headache or no headache.

To her relief the bright sky had clouded over, but the clouds soon grew so dark and threatening that a sudden, drenching shower overtook her as she arrived at the stop just in time to see her bus speeding out of sight.

Wondering bitterly what her horoscope could have been for the day, she tensed as a car horn honked behind her. Resigned, she turned to see the familiar red Daimler.

'Can I give you a lift?' called Alec, leaning out of the window. 'We're in for a storm; you'd better hop in.'

Much as Cassie would have preferred to refuse, common sense prevailed as she eyed the greenish black of the sky.

'Thank you,' she said, and slid into the passenger seat, lifting her wet hair away from her neck.

'There's a box of tissues under the dash,' said Alec.

Cassie mopped herself in silence as the car sped along the road in the teeth of the approaching storm. She flinched at a flash of lightning, then in seconds the world was a maelstrom of hail which pelted the car with such force that she was spared the need for polite conversation. By the time they reached Combe Cottage thunder was crashing overhead and rain enclosed the car in an impenetrable curtain.

'Thank you,' she said numbly as Alec leaned over to open the door.

'My pleasure. I won't get out. Sorry to rush you, but I'm due at Pennington General in five minutes.'

Cassie eyed him in consternation. 'You've come all this way only to go back again? I'd have waited for a bus if I'd known.'

'In *this*?' Alec waved a hand at the sodden, storm-lashed world outside, then turned suddenly to meet her eyes with a look which took her breath away. 'It's only sensible to make use of what shelter's available in a storm, Cassie.'

She blushed vividly and slid out of the car, racing through the rain to the house, careless of throbbing head and sore hand in her rush to get away from mocking blue eyes which told her that Alec Neville still possessed total recall of the last time they'd been caught together in a thunderstorm.

Cassie hurried upstairs to run a hot bath and strip

off her sodden clothes, not even noticing how much easier the process was now she was free of stitches and dressings. She let herself down into the steaming water with a sob of relief, eyes closed against the agony in her head, and at last let the videotape of her memory run through to the bitter end.

Alec Neville was no callow youth when he invaded Cassie Fletcher's life. She was his opposite in every way: introverted, wary of men, all her attention on her job in the path lab, where she combined on-the-job training with part-time studies. Alec was a sexually experienced, sophisticated man who swooped down on Cassie like the proverbial wolf on the fold the first time they met, then stopped short, the wind taken out of his sails when she looked up at him with unimpressed, velvet-dark eyes and silently handed him the results he was demanding.

When she finished work that evening Alec Neville was waiting outside, haggard, persuasive and very attractive to a wary Cassie, despite his outrageous hair and the earring. He demanded to see her again, wouldn't take no for an answer, and eventually, much against her better judgement, she gave in. Her initial antagonism towards him swiftly vanished, and soon they were seeing each other as often as they could, though often one or the other of them was obliged to cancel, on Alec's part because his job got in the way, on Cassie's for reasons she refused to give. To Alec she was a mystery he never solved. To Cassie he was the man she'd never even realised she'd dreamed of, and she accepted his 'no strings, no commitment' decree without protest, convincing herself that it was what she wanted too, that it would make things easier for them both when it ended, as it must, the moment Alec left Pennington for London at the end of the summer.

Cassie was soon fathoms-deep in love. All through that halcyon summer they snatched what time they could together, meeting for a snack or a drive in Alec's beloved old convertible, sometimes a trip to the cinema. But mostly they just walked along the riverbank, usually at sunset when the path was deserted. Alec spent so much time cooped up in an overheated hospital that he yearned for fresh air whenever he was free. Some Sundays they'd meet in the afternoon, take a picnic and a rug and talk and talk on every subject under the sun except the private life of Cassie Fletcher. They sought solitude with the feverish intensity of all lovers, and lay together under the trees, kissing wildly, their bodies on fire as Alec caressed her with such skill in his inflammatory hands that Cassie felt she'd die if she didn't give in to his urging. But, no matter how much Alec importuned and coaxed and grew desperate, she refused to let him make love to her in the way they both hungered for, conscious, always, of the fact that no possible permanence could be expected from their relationship.

Often Alec would tell her he was too old for all this, that kissing in the woods and in cars was for schoolboys, not responsible doctors, but Cassie would shrug and tell him the choice was his: the status quo or goodbye.

And all the time Cassie knew it was coming to an end, and tried not to think of it. Soon, all too soon, Alec would be gone. That last, fateful Sunday they'd been walking along their favourite stretch of river-bank, as usual too wrapped up in each other to notice much around them, so that when the wind rose and clouds blotted out the sun they were miles from the car when rain poured down and thunder cracked the sky in half. Lightning forked to earth all round them as Alec raced with her towards a derelict boat-house beside the river, where they wedged the drunken door shut against the elements and held each other close, breathing in agonised gasps, oblivious to cobwebs and the smell of old, rotting wood. Cassie's panic sub-sided, dispatched swiftly by dangerous, seductive heat which rose to bathe them in a common fire as their kisses grew wilder. Alec held her away from him, his eyes blazing as he saw her nipples pointing through the wet clinging T-shirt, and suddenly they were on their knees, their legs giving way to the force of their longing as he stripped the shirt over her head and snatched away the scraps of cotton protecting her breasts from his seeking mouth.

They collapsed in a heap on the dirty board floor, their bodies straining together as Alec tore off his clothes and the rest of Cassie's, and then he was over her and her breath was gone and he was inside her and she gave a sharp little moan at the sudden, burning pain and in a few short moments it was all over and he collapsed on her in shame, burrowing his wet dark head against her shoulder as Cassie sobbed bitterly, the salt tears running down her face and on to his as she struggled to get up. But Alec held her fast, straightening, stern-faced, to gaze down into her streaming eyes.

'No, Cassie. I won't let you go. Not like this. Darling, don't cry! It shouldn't have happened, but now it has, let me show you how it should be.' And he silenced her protesting mouth with his own and caressed her into submission, his hands so gentle that she relaxed gradually, her body still shaken by the occasional sob as he kissed and caressed every inch of it before invading it again, first with clever, searching fingers which made her gasp and surge against him, then with his body, as patiently and lovingly he taught her how it was meant to be when a man and a woman united in the experience they were created for. Cassie forgot her fear and pain, caught up in a mounting, convulsive pleasure which overwhelmed her so completely at the last that she cried out and clutched his bare shoulders, and Alec held her tightly as though he'd never let her go.

CHAPTER THREE

CASSIE came back to the present with a jolt, to cold bath-water and a heart throbbing more violently than her head. She yanked out the bath-plug and heaved herself to her feet to turn on the shower as cold as she could bear. Afterwards she pulled on a nightshirt and dressing-gown and, pleased she felt somewhat better, went downstairs in search of food. Cassie made tea and toast and poached an egg, then took her tray into the sitting-room and turned on the lamps against the subterranean gloom from the rain outside. She ate her meal slowly and absently, her mind occupied with the girl who'd made such a difficult, agonising decision after the experience in the boathouse all those years before.

After two days of torment she'd met Alec and told him, her throat thick with unshed tears, that although there was a month to go before he left for London she thought it best if they didn't see each other again. Cassie bit her lip as she remembered Alec's sudden, deathly pallor, the way his dark-ringed blue eyes had burned in his haggard, incredulous face.

He'd demanded explanations and reasons, but Cassie had refused to give any. No strings, no promises, just as he'd wanted, she'd reminded him brokenly. He was leaving soon, anyway. Better to make the break now—quickly and cleanly, before things got totally out of hand.

Alec, dizzy with lack of sleep and grief over a patient who'd died that day, had lost his temper, made wild accusations about another man, said a great many bitter, unforgivable things in his rage and hurt and stormed off back to the hospital, leaving Cassie alone by the riverbank feeling as though her heart had broken in so many pieces that it would never be whole again.

Where had she found the strength to send him away? she asked herself in wonder. She'd been so young, and so crazy about him. But early on in life she'd acquired an incurable suspicion of the entire male sex, and held a deep-rooted conviction that to continue with the relationship would result in disaster. Alec had been bluntly truthful from the first on the subject of responsibility and commitments. So that the young Cassie, who was threatened at the time with more than her share of both, felt she had no option but to shut Alec Neville out of her life.

Each time the telephone rang that evening Cassie leapt to answer it, embarrassed by her own disappointment when the callers were her mother and Ben, both of them enquiring after her hand now the stitches were out. You didn't really expect Alec to call, did you? she asked herself scornfully. He knows exactly how your hand is.

Nevertheless, when the phone rang a third time as she was on her way up to bed her heart gave a great thump at the sound of the voice she'd been hoping for.

'I know it's late to ask how you are, but I've been tied up all evening at the Burns Unit, Cassie,' said Alec. 'I've been worried about you. You looked desperately unwell this afternoon. I trust I'm not interrupting anything,' he added abruptly.

'No. I was just on my way to bed.'

'From the way you looked earlier you should already be there. Are you feeling better?'

'Yes. The head's settled down to a bearable throb.'

'And the hand?'

'A bit sore, but now the stitches are out I couldn't care less.'

He chuckled. 'Are you always such a baby about pain?'

'Not pain. Stitches.' She paused. 'It was kind of you to ring up, Alec. Are you as solicitous with all your patients?'

'No. Besides, you were Tom Parkinson's patient more than mine, Cassie. I prefer to think of you as a friend.' He paused. 'We were more than friends once upon a time, remember?'

As if she were ever likely to forget! 'It was a long time ago, Alec.'

'A mere lapse of time needn't veto a resumption of friendship, Cassie.' He paused. 'But I forgot. Your inspector forbids it.'

Cassie stiffened. 'I'm long past the age when any-one forbids me anything, Alec!'

'Good. Then perhaps we might meet one evening for that meal I suggested.' He paused. 'You're a mys-tery I'd very much like to solve. Your inspector should have sympathy with that, surely—right up his street!'

'A touch of mystery adds to a woman's charm, surely,' she countered.

'You need no help on that score, Cassie.' Alec paused. 'Now you're no longer my patient, why not have dinner with me this coming weekend—for old times' sake?'

Cassie thought about it. After their quarrel the night before she had no idea about Liam's plans for the weekend. Probably he was spending the day with the twins again, anyway. 'All right,' she said quickly, be-fore she could change her mind. 'Saturday?'

'Good. I'll call for you at seven-thirty.'

'I could drive to meet you somewhere now I've got two hands.'

'No, Cassie. I'll come for you. Goodnight. Sleep well.'

When Cassie was finally in bed the phone rang again.

'I know it's late, Cassie,' said Liam's voice wea-rily, 'but your bloody phone's been engaged all eve-ning. I thought I'd have one last try before I got some sleep.'

'Hello, Liam,' she said politely, still smarting from their quarrel.

'Look, Cassie, I'm sorry. About last night, I mean.' He waited. 'Are you still there?'

'Yes.'

'You're a very lovely lady, Cassie—you can't blame a chap for trying.'

'I don't. But I insist on the right to say no, Liam. Anyway, apology accepted—let's forget it.'

'Anything you say. Can I come round tomorrow night?'

'Of course. I'll make dinner—again.'

He chuckled wryly. 'And this time I'll eat it. I was hoping to spend most of the weekend with you, but I've got the twins again. I won't ask you to put up with them two weeks running.'

'Detta going shopping again?' asked Cassie tartly.

'Shopping? No, actually she's a bit under the weather and her mother's away, so I'm taking them off her hands for the weekend.'

'Good for you. See you tomorrow, then.'

'Wait a minute, Cassie—who were you talking to all night on the phone?'

'Just my mother and Ben and so on. They called to ask after my hand. I had the stitches out today,' she added pointedly.

'Oh, hell, so you did. It slipped my mind. Sorry, Cassie, everything OK?'

'Just fine. Goodnight, Liam.'

Cassie decided to defer getting down to work again

until after the weekend, and spent next day gardening in sunshine, which made a welcome contrast to the storm of the day before. Her mood was buoyant as she grubbed happily in the damp earth, something she put down to the absence of her famous stitches. Not to mention the fact that you're entertaining one man to dinner tonight and dining out with another tomorrow, you fast hussy, she reminded herself gleefully.

When Liam arrived Cassie's welcome was noticeably restrained.

'Don't worry, I won't jump on you,' he said drily, and kissed her cheek with pointed care as he handed her a bottle of wine, chuckling when Cassie explained her approval of wine rather than chocolates.

The evening progressed pleasantly enough until Liam enquired about the identity of the man who'd driven his daughters home the previous Saturday.

'Detta said it was a very impressive car,' he remarked, 'and the driver was obviously on pretty familiar terms with you.'

Cassie shrugged. 'You weren't around to take Kitty and Tess home and I couldn't get a taxi. Alec Neville, Tom Parkinson's successor, happened to be passing, so he kindly gave your daughters a lift.'

Liam scowled. 'Happened to be passing—in Combe Aston? Come off it, Cass!'

She eyed him levelly. 'He was touring the district looking at houses for sale, and happened to be driving up the lane when I was playing ball in the garden with the twins. More coffee?'

'No, thanks.' He gave her a hostile stare. 'Look, Cassie, in future I'd rather you didn't involve my daughters with strangers.'

Cassie glared back, struggling to keep her temper. 'Alec isn't a stranger to *me*. Besides, your transport arrangements had rather broken down, if you remember. And, much as I'm fond of Kitty and Tess, I hadn't been expecting to have them at all last Saturday, Liam. You took me very much for granted.'

He got up slowly, his bulk overpowering the low-ceilinged room. 'Then there's not much point in asking you to come out with us this Saturday too, I take it?'

'No. I've made other plans.'

'What plans?' he asked sharply.

Cassie jumped to her feet, disliking the feeling of being loomed over. 'It's not actually your business what I do when you're not around, you know, Liam.'

'My mistake! I thought it was.'

They glowered at each other in silence, then Cassie sighed impatiently. 'We're quarrelling again.'

Liam relaxed a little, managing a reluctant grin. 'So we are. Let's kiss and make up before I go.'

Cassie went into his arms, smiling brightly to hide her sudden, dismayed reluctance, but when his mouth closed hungrily on hers it took all the self-control she possessed to stay put. Liam's arms dropped at last and he stepped back.

'I'm still not forgiven.'

'Of course you are,' she assured him. 'Give me a

ring to let me know what nights you're free next week. I know I usually leave my socialising for weekends, but there's a good comedy on at the Playhouse. As I'm not seeing you on Saturday, let's go one night in the week.'

Liam's dark face brightened a little. 'Wednesday or Thursday should be OK. Book some tickets and I'll settle up when I buy you supper afterwards.'

'Done!'

Cassie took a long time to get to sleep after Liam had gone, disturbed by the discovery that not only was there no question of his becoming her lover, it was an effort to allow him even a goodnight kiss. Tonight he'd assumed she was still cool after their quarrel, but next time she'd have no excuse. And it was nothing to do with Liam himself. Unaware of his culpability he might be, but the blame, nevertheless, was Alec Neville's.

The following evening Cassie found herself taking a great deal more trouble with her appearance than usual in preparation for her evening with Alec. She tamed her hair ruthlessly, securing the gleaming golden-brown curls at the nape of her neck with a black silk scarf, then she put on a sleeveless black linen dress, added a hip-length white jacket and heavy silver spiral earrings, and emphasised her eyes and lips rather more than she normally did. The result, she decided, eyeing herself in a full-length mirror, wasn't bad at all.

Alec Neville was obviously in full agreement, his eyes openly appreciative when Cassie opened her door to him.

'Cassie, you look wonderful!'

'Why, thank you.' She smiled, her heart giving an errant thump under the black linen as she waved a hand at his elegant dark suit. 'So do you. Won't you come in for a drink?'

He shot back a gleaming white shirt-cuff to consult his watch. 'No time really. If you're ready we'll be off. I had to do some persuading to get them to give me a table at short notice, so we'd better be on the dot.'

Cassie locked her door and accompanied her tall, imposing escort down the garden path, surprised by a rush of pleasure so intense that it rang alarm bells in her head as Alec handed her into the car.

'You look so much better than when I saw you last that I hardly recognise you,' he commented as he got in beside her.

'I'm not surprised,' she said cheerfully. 'Happily, this is more me than the patient you dealt with on Thursday.'

'Looking back on it, I can't say I remember you with as much as a sniffle in the old days.'

'True. I missed only three weeks' work at the path lab all the time I was there—' Cassie halted, biting her lip.

'I remember the occasion,' he said without inflexion.

She frowned 'How?'

'I went looking for you. But I was told you were taking some time off due to illness. What was wrong with you, Cassie?'

'The illness wasn't mine.'

He gave her a swift glance then returned his attention to the road. 'Cassie, now I've met you again my curiosity has revived in full force about what happened all those years ago. I won't insult your intelligence by pretending I've spent all the intervening years wondering about it. In fact at first I tried my damnedest to put you from my mind and pretend I'd never met you. It wasn't easy. I'd hear a song we liked, or get a whiff of the perfume you used, and I'd be transported straight back to that summer to rack my brains as to why it ended the way it did.' His mouth twisted satirically. 'How my ego suffered!'

'Probably did you the world of good,' said Cassie callously, then gave him a wry little smile. 'But I promise I'll sing for my supper. After all, it's the sole reason you asked me out tonight.'

'Not quite.' He returned the smile in kind as he parked the car in front of the Chesterton, the largest hotel in Pennington. He turned in his seat to look at her. 'Do you still find it painful to talk about?'

Cassie shook her head. 'No. Not any more.'

His hard blue eyes softened. 'Good.'

She looked at him thoughtfully. 'Ten years is a long time, Alec. I was sure you'd have forgotten all about me by now.'

'Had you forgotten about me?'

'No.'

'Then why the surprise that I still remember?'

'Because whenever I thought of you I pictured you far too busy scaling the medical heights to have time to think of anything else.'

Alec shook his head. 'Don't under-rate yourself, Cassie. Quite apart from the fact that you're the only woman who ever gave me my marching orders, you were—still are—a very memorable lady.'

'And at the moment,' she said lightly, 'I'm a very hungry one.'

Alec smiled, taking his cue from her as he walked with her into the hotel which had been the town's most luxurious watering place since Pennington first became fashionable as a spa.

Cassie had never been treated to dinner at the Chesterton before and thoroughly enjoyed the atmosphere of relaxed, effortless comfort. She studied the complicated menu with unconcealed pleasure, and looked up after a while to find Alec watching her with a strange look in his eyes.

'What is it?' she asked. 'Smut on my nose?'

He shook his head. 'No. I just find it hard to credit the change in you, Cassie. Your face is so expressive these days. When you were young you hid behind a very effective mask.'

'Perhaps if you'd brought me here to eat I'd have shown more animation,' she parried lightly.

'On the salary I earned then you were lucky to get a cheeseburger!'

'Don't remind me.' She pulled a face. 'After we broke up I could never look one in the face again.'

'Is that true, Cassie?' he asked swiftly.

She nodded, then drank some of her wine, her pulse quickening at the look in his eyes.

'So what would you like instead?' he asked. 'Since I last knew you, fashions have changed in food. Anything you won't eat?'

'Several things, but no categories.' She smiled quizzically. 'As tonight's by way of a one-off occasion, would it presume on old acquaintance too much to ask for lobster Newburg?'

'Why should it be a one-off? Which doesn't mean you can't have your lobster—or anything your heart desires,' he assured her, and beckoned the hovering waiter.

They talked with less constraint than Cassie had expected, finding common ground on almost every topic as she applied herself with frank enjoyment to her meal.

'It's wonderful to have both hands free to eat,' she said with satisfaction.

'Were you suffering by the time you had the operation?'

'Not suffering, exactly, except from inconvenience. I type a lot in my line of work and a dead hand interfered with that no end.' Cassie grimaced. 'When it began to keep me awake at night as well I had no option, much as I dreaded the whole thing.'

'You work in an office?' asked Alec curiously.

'In a way—but, talking of work, I'd love to hear more about yours.'

For the rest of the meal Cassie listened, deeply interested, as Alec told her about his stint at University Hospital, London, and how he'd seized on the opportunity to specialise in plastic surgery when it was offered him.

'Though it irritates me when people assume I do nothing but operate on wealthy women desperate to look younger,' he said, over coffee. 'Mostly I rebuild faces after accidents, remove facial tumours and so on, and, of course, there's my work in the Burns Unit. But my particular speciality is microsurgery, with the emphasis on hands.' He smiled across at her. 'You should have hung on a bit longer, Cassie. I could have done your carpal tunnel myself.'

'Would you have given me a cut-rate for an old friend?' she asked blithely, then could have kicked herself as he smiled very deliberately into her eyes.

'I might even have done it for love, Cassie.'

'Highly unethical,' she said briskly, hoping her heightened colour was masked by the dim lighting. 'The labourer's worthy of his hire, Alec. I was perfectly happy to cough up your consultation fee.'

She changed the subject and began to discuss a novel that was making the current headlines, and soon they were deep in an argument on the merits of the writer, enjoying their verbal sparring.

Though this was less of a surprise than it might have been, reflected Cassie later in the cloakroom. When they were young the only time they'd stopped talking was to make love. She breathed in sharply, meeting her arrested eyes in the mirror. This time round, she warned her reflection, keep to conversation. Your heart mended once. It might not manage it a second time.

They drove back through an evening so bright with moonlight that Combe Cottage looked fey and unreal when Alec stopped the car at the gate.

'How long have you lived here, Cassie?'

'Just over two years.' She sighed with satisfaction. 'I just love it.'

'Are you never lonely?'

'Too busy to be lonely.'

He looked up and down the deserted lane, then back at the house. 'Nevertheless it's very isolated here, Cassie—you could do with some security lights, at least.'

'And spoil the charm of the cottage? No way! Now then, would you like this coffee I wouldn't give you the other night?'

'As long as you understand it isn't only coffee I want,' Alec said mockingly. 'The other requirement, of course, being nothing more sinister than the talk you promised me.'

'What else?' she said lightly, refusing to rise. She

preceded him up the path to unlock the door, switched on some lamps, then beckoned him inside.

Alec stood in the middle of her sitting-room, his head not far short of the central beam. His eyes moved slowly over the comfortable, chintz-covered furniture, the book-crammed shelves flanking the recessed fireplace, the copper bowl of tawny chrysanthemums screening the empty fire-basket. 'Last time I was too busy wondering if the twins were yours to notice the décor. All your own work, Cassie?'

'My taste down to the last cushion,' she assured him, removing her jacket.

'Tell me to mind my own business,' he said, frowning, 'but, small though it is, this house must have cost quite a bit, and your furniture's good. That Pembroke table over there's a very nice piece. Did you come into money, Cassie?'

'I was given the down-payment when my grandmother's house was sold, but I pay off the mortgage by the sweat of my brow.' She smiled. 'Make yourself at home while I see to the coffee. Care for a brandy with it?'

He shook his head regretfully. 'I'd better not.'

'There's a compact disc player hiding in that cabinet under the window. Choose some music, if you like, I won't be long.'

When Cassie returned from the kitchen with a coffee tray the strains of Ravel's *Daphnis et Chloë* were stealing through the room.

Alec sprang up to take the tray from her. 'I like your taste in music, Cassie.'

'The CD player's a very new toy. I don't have much to play on it yet.' She waved him to the sofa, poured coffee, then kicked off her shoes and curled up in the big chair opposite him. 'Do you like my house, Alec?'

'I admire it,' he said obliquely. 'And I can see now why you've never married. A man would need pretty powerful inducement to lure you away from this.'

'True. And it's too small to ask anyone to move in to share it.'

'Have you ever considered that?'

'Only once, but it didn't prove practical.'

'You mean the good inspector, or the almost husband?'

Cassie looked at him levelly. 'Neither.'

Alec met the look, then drained his coffee-cup and put it down. 'All right, Cassie. Let's make a pact. You tell me as much about yourself as you're prepared to, and if you're interested I'll return the compliment. Though,' he added drily, 'I can't say you've shown the same interest in my private life as I have in yours. After that point we'll let the past go, agreed?'

'Agreed,' she said promptly. 'What would you like to know first?'

'How about telling me what you do for a living these days?'

'Right. Come with me.' Cassie got up, slid her feet into her shoes and led the way from the sitting-room and into her office. '*Voilà*,' she said, succumbing to drama. 'This is where I work. I'm afraid the décor doesn't match the rest of the house.'

Alec Neville halted on the threshold of the small room, his eyes narrowing as he took in the word processor on a battered leather-topped table, the functional steel filing cabinet. The walls were lined with shelves, some of them stacked with works of fiction, others with reference books of all kinds, many of them concerned with various aspects of crime. On the wall above the desk a small framed award hung beside a noticeboard with notes and cuttings and photographs pinned to it. A separate bookshelf just inside the door was reserved solely for the works of one author, obviously thrillers by the design of the dust jackets but only four of the volumes in English, the rest in various foreign languages.

'Quinn Fletcher?' said Alec, thunderstruck. '*You're* Quinn Fletcher?'

'The very same,' said Cassie. 'My mother's maiden name was Quinn.'

He whistled softly in amazement. 'I saw one of your books only this morning, in my local newsagent's.'

'And you never knew it was little old me!'

'Sincere congratulations, Cassie. I'm delighted for you.' Alec eyed the display of books with respect. 'I'm not addicted to the genre myself but I'll make an exception in your case.'

'I should hope so!' Cassie smiled. 'Let's go back

to the other room and get comfortable. Instead of giving you bits and pieces you may as well hear the story from the beginning.' She eyed him challengingly. 'That's if you're sure you want it all.'

Alec held her eyes very deliberately. 'Of course I want it all, Cassie. I always did.'

CHAPTER FOUR

CASSIE stared at him, transfixed for a moment, then turned abruptly and went into the other room, busying herself with pouring more coffee and fluffing up the cushions in the armchair before she curled up in it again. With her eyes fixed firmly on the flowers in the fireplace, she asked Alec where he'd like her to begin.

'At the beginning. Everything from the day you were born,' he said promptly.

Cassie shook her head. 'No need to go back that far. My early childhood was uneventful, spent in a nice, ordinary house on the outskirts of Pennington. My father was manager of a small construction firm there. Life was comfortable and pleasant until just after my sixteenth birthday, when my father was offered a better job with a firm in Birmingham.'

When Richard Fletcher went to the new post, however, he had left his family behind, leaving his shell-shocked wife to explain to Cassie and her eight-year-old brother that their father wanted a divorce so he could marry his secretary. Hiding her grief valiantly, Kate Fletcher had made it clear to her children that their father wanted them to visit him as often as possible once he was settled.

'Did you go?' asked Alec.

Cassie shook her head. 'No fear! Sixteen is rarely anyone's most tolerant stage of development. I was utterly disgusted. Pauline, the secretary, was only twenty-four. To me my father was *old*. Far too old to be sleeping with a girl in her twenties—or anyone else.' She smiled wryly. 'Actually he was only forty-eight, my mother a mere thirty-nine.'

'Had she known what he had in mind?'

'No. One minute she was secure in her marriage, then the next, wham! It was all over. She told me later that the first thing she knew of it was when Dad said he was off.'

Kate Fletcher had fought hard to make the best of things for her children, but worse was to come. Her husband had promised she wouldn't suffer financially, but only a few weeks after leaving his wife and family he had died suddenly of a heart attack.

'Father hadn't got as far as making a will,' said Cassie, 'so at least his life insurance went to Mother. But otherwise his double life had taken all his cash. Unknown to Mother, he'd taken out a second mortgage on our house. My mother sold it for what little she could get, and rented a much smaller one.' She flushed. 'You probably remember it.'

'Vividly,' observed Alec, poker-faced. 'Tell me the rest.'

Cassie did her best to be brief as she completed her story. Kate had brushed up on her secretarial skills and found a job. Cassie had abandoned her plans for university and gone to work in the path lab instead when she left school. Young Ben, bewildered and unhappy by his father's desertion, had nevertheless adjusted more quickly to the situation. As long as he had Cassie and his mother, Ben could cope.

'Did *you* cope?' asked Alec.

'In my own way. My reaction was a total loathing and distrust of the entire male sex. I had a boyfriend at the time, a fellow sixth former, totally harmless, but Dad did so much damage to me emotionally that I sent David packing. No man was ever going to hurt me the way my father hurt my mother.'

'Which explains a lot,' said Alec grimly. 'Though not everything. If you were so against men, why did you let *me* into your life?'

Cassie looked at him very directly. 'I didn't intend to, but I just couldn't help it. You—you were different. And at the time I badly needed what we had together. Not just the lovemaking, though I wanted that as much as you did. It was the companionship, the rapport we had. I literally lived for the times we spent together.'

Alec got up suddenly and pulled her to her feet, leading her back to the sofa to sit beside him. 'So why the devil did you keep me separate from your family?'

'I was very young, remember. Young enough to be ashamed of my home after hearing about yours. And on top of that I couldn't bring myself to trust in you completely after what happened with my father. I was a fairly mixed-up kid at that time. But, more important than all that, Mother was so ill,' finished Cassie simply. 'I didn't want to involve you.'

Alec frowned, plainly trying for patience. 'Hell, Cassie, I'm a doctor. What difference would that have made to me?'

'Ah, but you told me from the first that there was no room in your life for responsibilities and ties. And you were about to take off for London, remember.' She turned to look at him. 'I'm not talking flu or appendicitis. Mother had serious thyroid problems— Graves' disease. She became so ill that my grandmother moved in to let me keep my job at the lab.'

'Did your mother know about me?'

'Yes, of course. Both she and Gran were delighted I was getting over Dad enough to have a boyfriend at last.'

'So what happened?' he prompted gently.

'When I got home that Sunday after—after the storm, my mother was worse. She was admitted next day, so Ben and I moved in with Gran because her house was much nearer the hospital. She'd always wanted us to live with her once Dad went, anyway.' Cassie took in a deep breath. 'Mother was terribly ill, Alec; on the danger-list for a while. The path lab gave me compassionate leave.'

'Bloody hell, Cassie—why couldn't you have *told* me?' he demanded savagely.

'What was I to say? You didn't want responsibility. I was up to my neck in it. And my grandmother was old. My father's parents were dead. If Mother had died too I was all Ben had. How could I load you with all that?'

His fingers tightened on hers. 'Did your mother recover, Cassie?'

'Yes, in time. She's a fighter. She not only recovered, she married the man she used to work for. Michael Whitley was a widower who decided to retire early and take her off to live in a house overlooking Cardigan Bay. She's had a new lease of life—in more ways than one.'

There was silence in the room for a while after Cassie finished, for so long that she began to fidget, tried to take her hand away, but Alec held on to it firmly.

'And you kept me totally in the dark,' he said at last. 'I suppose you heard about my visit to Alma Street, Cassie? I bullied one of your colleagues into giving me your address, but there was no answer at the house when I knocked. When I asked one of your neighbours for information she told me you were away and got rid of me at top speed.'

Cassie giggled suddenly. 'If you mean Mrs Platt, she strongly disapproved of the hair and the earring, not to mention that scruffy old leather jacket. She told me she was sure I didn't want nothing to do with a nasty type like that.'

'She made her opinion very plain,' he said acidly.

Cassie gave him a long, level look. 'At least you found out why I wouldn't let you come to see me in

Alma Street. I knew it was all Mother could afford, but that didn't stop me from being ashamed of it.'

Alec snorted. 'Did you think I'd have cared a toss what your house was like?'

'*I* cared!'

'What a silly little idiot you were, Cassie Fletcher.'

'I know that now,' she agreed ruefully, then smiled. 'Funny, really. If I still lived in Alma Street I'd invite you there without a qualm. Something to do with growing up, I suppose.'

Alec's grip tightened on the hand she tried to withdraw. 'Purely academic, of course, after all this time, but if it hadn't been for your mother and Ben would you have come away with me if I'd asked you, Cassie?'

She stared at him, startled, then shrugged. 'How can I tell? You were pretty blunt about it never being a possibility. I would have wanted to, desperately. But after what happened with my father I doubt I'd have said yes—even to someone I cared about, like you.'

He nodded grimly. 'Just as I thought. But you could have answered my note, surely.'

'What note?'

'The one I left with the formidable Mrs Platt.'

Cassie frowned. 'She never said anything about a note, Alec.'

His eyes hardened. 'Are you saying that venomous old harpy didn't give it to you?'

'I didn't see her for weeks. She probably forgot.'

She looked at him questioningly. 'What did the note say?'

'Not much. Just a demand to see you. I was off my head with worry. I was pretty sure you didn't take the Pill and you know damn well I didn't take any precautions that day. The thought of you alone and pregnant gave me nightmares.'

Cassie's eyes lit with sudden, amused comprehension. 'Oh, I see now—that's why you looked so shattered when you saw me with Liam's twins!'

'Confronted by two little charmers of exactly the right age and colouring, do you blame me?' He frowned. 'But Cassie, I wrote again—twice—when I found a flat. Still no answer, so in the end I gave up. Rejection was a new experience, and bloody hard to take.'

Cassie thought for a moment. 'By then we must have left forty-four Alma Street and gone to live with my grand-mother—'

'What number did you say?' he interrupted.

'All the fours, forty-four.'

'I thought you lived at *thirty*-four.'

They stared at each other for a moment.

'I wondered why you spoke to Mrs Platt,' said Cassie slowly. 'She lived a fair way up the street. Number thirty-four was sold about the same time as we left ours. The new people wouldn't have known us—they probably just threw the letters away.' She sighed. 'Fate was against us all the way, Alec.'

They sat in thoughtful silence for a while.

'Yet Fate's relented sufficiently to let us meet up again,' Alec said at last.

Cassie withdrew her hand firmly. 'Probably to let us satisfy our curiosity. Would you like some more coffee?'

'No. I've yet to hear what—or who—effected the transformation in Cassie Fletcher.' Alec swept a look from the crown of her head to the tips of her toes. 'You're a very different person from the girl I knew— and it's nothing to do with the ten-year gap. Somewhere along the way you came to terms with life, Cassie.'

She nodded soberly. 'I did. It began the day I learned my mother would recover. A great load rolled off my shoulders and my entire perspective on life began to shift. Just to have her alive was so miraculous that I began to lose my bitterness about my father. In time I even learned to live with the pain of losing you. Though after you'd gone I couldn't bear to go back to my old job. I applied for one in the forensic laboratory instead, joined a health club, went to creative-writing classes in the evenings, and eventually stopped saying no when perfectly nice men asked me out.'

A shadow darkened Alec's face. 'While for me the only thing that kept me sane those first few weeks in London, Cassie, was the memory of your face as you sent me away.'

'Why?'

'I took some comfort—when I could think

straight—from the fact that, whatever your reasons
were, you were no more happy about ending it than
I was.'

'Happy!' She gave a mirthless laugh. 'When you
stormed off that day it felt like the end of the world.
I was utterly heartbroken.'

Alec studied her face closely. 'But your heart obviously mended, Cassie.'

'Oh, yes, it mended.' She slanted a look at him.
'Odd, though, it never occurred to me that you'd be
worried about repercussions from—from the boat-
house episode.'

'Surely you were worried yourself?'

'No. I knew quite soon that there wasn't anything
to worry about—on that score anyway. For which I
was deeply grateful. It was one less complication in
a life which had worries enough at the time.' She
jumped to her feet. 'Right. Enough soul-searching for
one night, Alec.'

He got up at once. 'You mean it's time for me to
go.'

'Yes,' she said candidly, and took any sting from
her words with her smile. 'It was a gorgeous dinner
and I enjoyed the evening very much, but all this
catharsis is a bit draining. I'm tired!'

'Then I'll say goodnight, Cassie. Thank you for
clearing up the mystery at last.' He looked at her for
a moment, then caught her in his arms and kissed her
surprised, parted mouth. Then he gathered her closer
and kissed her again, and went on kissing her at such

length that they were both breathing heavily when he finally released her.

'I knew it!' he exclaimed, his voice husky with desire.

She stared up at him, dazed. 'What do you mean?'

'The chemistry between us hasn't changed in the slightest.' Alec reached out a hand to touch her flushed cheek. 'Goodnight, Cassie.' He walked with her to the door, then stood for a moment, looking down at her. 'I've found a house, by the way.'

Blinking, Cassie pulled herself together. 'Really? Where?'

'In Beaufort Square, on the north side of Pennington. It's Georgian, in good condition and big enough to allow for consulting-rooms on the ground floor.' He moved closer. 'When I've moved in, come and see it.'

'Thank you. I'd like to.' Her smile faded as she saw the sudden heat in his eyes, and she put out her hands in a warding-off motion. 'No, Alec—'

'Yes, Cassie,' he said inexorably, and pulled her to him, stifling her protests with his mouth in the way she remembered so well. The ten years melted away and she was twenty years old and every inch of her burning with response to Alec Neville's touch.

When he raised his head his eyes blazed with triumph. 'Give me one good reason why two consenting adults shouldn't kiss each other!'

'Because in this instance only one of them's consenting!' She pulled free sharply, pushing at a falling lock of hair as she scowled at him. 'You can't expect to—to just take up where we left off after all this time, Alec!'

'Why not?' he demanded with characteristic arrogance.

'For all I know you could have a wife and family waiting somewhere, ready to move into your new house!'

'I haven't. I told you I don't have a wife any more,' he said brusquely, but when he reached for her again Cassie dodged out of his reach.

'No, Alec. I'm not twenty and vulnerable any more.'

For a moment his eyes glinted cold with anger, then he shrugged indifferently.

'But apparently still the same little tease underneath the new veneer. You haven't really changed at all, Cassie.'

'In some ways,' she agreed with dangerous calm, 'I haven't.'

'In that case I'll say goodnight. Coy sexual games are not to my taste these days.' He smiled at the flash of outrage in her eyes before she controlled it. 'Not,' he added, 'that my evening was wasted.'

'Good.' Cassie's dark eyes flashed coldly. 'You can sleep easy now the mystery's solved, Alec, your ego intact. You were never actually rejected after all.'

Alec stood looking at her for a moment longer then inclined his head formally, thanked her for her company, and strode out of the house, leaving Cassie flat and depressed, wondering whether she'd been incredibly sensible or incredibly foolish.

Ben Fletcher came round next day to lunch, which meant Cassie spent most of her time preparing food, cooking it, or clearing it away, though to be fair her brother lent a hand at all stages. As always he made her laugh a lot, the eight-year gap between them almost non-existent now Ben had a job with the electronics firm who'd sponsored him through university. As they ate the roast Cassie usually cooked for Ben she outlined the plot of her new novel to him, picking his brains now and then as she scribbled on the notebook always kept at the ready.

'Though I should think Liam would be more use to you than me,' said Ben, as he got ready to go.

'Only on the technicalities. I needed a bit of male emotional reaction. Not his strong point. Besides, I haven't seen much of Liam lately.' Cassie shrugged. 'These days I come way down on his list of priorities.'

Ben eyed her curiously. 'Do I spot a note of discord?'

She shook her head, smiling. 'No, not at all—' She looked up as the telephone rang, and Ben bent to give her a swift peck on the cheek.

'I'll leave you to your policeman and dash—got someone waiting.'

Cassie laughed, waving him off as she picked up the phone.

'You sound very chirpy,' said Liam.

Then I'm a better actress than I thought, reflected Cassie, as she told him Ben was responsible for her cheerful mood. She enquired after the twins, refrained from being bitchy about Detta's health, then grimaced, unseen, when Liam asked if she'd booked for the theatre. She promised to arrange it right away, not daring to admit she'd forgotten. Liam was touchy enough lately as it was. She made a mental note to finish earlier on the day to make sure she stayed awake during the play.

During the week that followed Cassie was deeply grateful for the absorbing nature of the work. For the major part of the day it occupied her to the point where she could successfully put Alec Neville to the back of her mind. The evenings and nights were another matter.

Once work was over for the day, all Cassie could think of was Alec. Her behaviour had been perfectly correct towards him, she assured herself. Alec had no right to expect her to fall into his arms like a ripe plum after all this time, even if their parting *had* been none of his own doing. Whatever he said, she was a different woman now from the inhibited, suspicious Cassie of ten years before. But the transition to her present calm control of her fate hadn't been won overnight, and she had no intention of risking its loss for anyone. Having experienced heartbreak over Alec once, she had no taste for a second dose of the same medicine. She would have liked to resume some kind of relationship with him, she knew only too well. But with Alec mere friendship obviously wasn't possible. The physical chemistry between them was too inflammable for that. But a love-affair was out of the question. She liked her life the way it was—or how it had been before Alec Neville's re-entry into it.

To say Cassie was annoyed was an understatement when Liam rang early on the Thursday evening to say he couldn't make it to the theatre after all. It took effort to assure him it didn't matter, and Cassie somehow managed to refrain from telling him that the time wasted in getting ready could have been far better employed on plotting D.S. Harriet Gale's progress on the trail of a serial killer.

Cassie dialled her brother's number irritably and offered him the two tickets for the theatre. 'I'm sure there's some gorgeous creature you can take with you.' She was saying no more than the truth. Ben Fletcher never lacked feminine company.

'There certainly is,' said Ben promptly. 'You, Cassie.'

'*Me*?'

'Why not? You were all set to go anyway. I'll even stand you supper afterwards in the theatre restaurant—I got paid today.'

'You're on! I'll meet you in the circle bar in an hour.'

The play was a very witty comedy. Cassie thoroughly enjoyed the first two acts, glad she'd made the effort to drive into town after all. During the second

interval she went off with Ben to the bar, and met up
with a trio of colleagues from his firm eager to be
introduced to his clever, attractive sister. The talk was
animated and light-hearted as Cassie drank her glass
of wine, then the bell rang and Ben slid an arm round
her waist to shepherd her through the crowd, bending
down to whisper in her ear, 'There's a tall, dark guy
over there looking daggers at you, Cass.'

She stood on tiptoe to look through the crowd into
a pair of hard blue eyes which swept her up and down
then took stock of her companion before Alec Neville
nodded curtly and turned back to the maturely attractive blonde at his side.

'Friend of yours?' said Ben as they took their seats.

'Used to be,' muttered Cassie, and looked up from
the programme to see Alec and his blonde companion
entering one of the boxes with a group of people,
among them Mr Parkinson, his predecessor.

'If looks could kill I'd be on a slab in the morgue
by now,' whispered Ben, following her eyes. 'If you
ask me, the man's jealous.'

'Rubbish! Anyway, I wasn't asking you,' she retorted crossly.

'Probably thinks I'm your toyboy,' hissed Ben, and
to Cassie's horror he slid his arm round her shoulders
and pressed a lingering kiss on her hair.

Fortunately the house lights went down at that
point. Cassie stared unseeingly at the stage for the
rest of the performance, and the moment the curtain
came down rushed Ben out of the theatre and into the

car park at top speed, desperate to avoid another encounter with Alec.

'I thought I was taking you to supper,' complained Ben as his sister hustled him to her car.

'You can settle for fish and chips at your place and like it after your jolly jape in there, my boy,' she said tersely.

Ben eyed her in contrition as she drove off. 'Only a joke, Cass. Hope I didn't throw a spanner in the works.'

Cassie calmed down. 'It was quite funny really,' she admitted after a while, and refused to talk about it any more while they collected a take-away to eat in Ben's chronically chaotic flat. When Cassie got home she switched on her answerphone gingerly, but the only message on it was from her mother, assuring her daughter that it was only her weekly chat, and for Cassie to ring back when she could. 'I hope you're out enjoying yourself somewhere, darling. Mike sends his love and so do I.'

Cassie sighed. She had enjoyed herself, until she'd seen Alec. Who, she thought crossly, was the double-breasted blonde? She went to bed in an advanced state of irritation, reminding herself that neither she nor Alec had the least right to get annoyed about the other's social life, even if they had been lovers briefly, long ago in the past. Not only were they ten years older, hopefully they were ten years wiser, too.

CHAPTER FIVE

CASSIE began to regret her repudiation of Alec's love-making as the days went by without any word from him. What had she expected? she asked herself irritably. Alec was the last man to take a second rejection kindly. Not that she'd meant to reject him, exactly. Her resistance had been more in the line of letting him know she wasn't ready to fall into his arms merely for the asking. Alec Neville was a mature, experienced man who would naturally expect to be her lover. And a relationship of that nature wasn't something she was ready to trust herself to yet, even with Alec. Or did she mean especially with Alec? He was a very different man from the young registrar she'd known before. And somewhere along the line, she reminded herself, he'd acquired and lost a wife.

Fortunately, she had more than her usual absorption in her writing to take her mind off Alec for the moment. Quite apart from getting on with her crime novel, Cassie was also preparing a talk she'd been asked to give at the Pennington Literary Festival on her own particular method of tackling her work, and how she'd come to start writing on crime in the first place.

Unfortunately Ben was away on a course, and Liam

was uncertain whether he could make it that night, which meant that Cassie set off for the Chesterton that Friday feeling a little nervous with no prospect of a familiar face in the audience for support. She smiled wryly as she parked her car. A second free dinner at the best hotel in town in such a short space of time was a very unexpected occurrence. And she was obliged to sing for her supper again tonight, though hopefully to a larger audience than before.

Wearing the same black dress, but this time topped by a striped beige and black jacket, with a black silk handkerchief in her breast pocket and plain pearl studs in her ears, Cassie hoped the result was businesslike as well as attractive as she could make it. From the smile the festival organiser gave her when she walked into the foyer she was confident she'd achieved her aim, as he introduced her to various peo ple involved in the organisation of the festival before ushering her straight into dinner so that they could finish well in time before the hour appointed for Cassie's talk. After the meal she was hurried off to the ballroom, where a gratifyingly large crowd had gathered to hear her speak. On the small stage a lavish flower arrangement on an easel stood to one side of a table which held microphones and the usual carafe and glasses for water. Ian Selby, the organiser, led her to a chair behind the table, then stood beside her, waiting expectantly until the room was quiet and he was able to introduce Miss Quinn Fletcher. He made a few introductory remarks, then Cassie rose to her feet to encouraging applause, holding the notes she'd prepared.

Once she'd begun Cassie forgot her nerves and began to enjoy herself. Her study of drama and elocution in school stood her in good stead, and she knew she'd managed to capture the interest of the audience almost from the start. Taking care not to make the lecture too long, she did her best to make it entertaining, and had her reward with prolonged, appreciative applause when she finally resumed her seat. Ian Selby thanked her warmly, then invited questions, which came so thick and fast from the audience that he was obliged to end the session twenty minutes later than scheduled, so that Cassie could indulge in a hectic session of signing, as she autographed the pile of paperback books brought along by the local bookshop to sell to members of the audience.

'One last copy,' said Ian Selby, 'and you shall have the drink you deserve.'

Cassie pulled the last paperback towards her and said, 'What name shall I put?' She looked up with a smile, which grew fixed as she met a very familiar pair of blue eyes.

'Ah, Mr Neville, nice to see you here,' said Ian Selby, smiling deferentially. 'Have you met Miss Fletcher?'

Alec smiled down at Cassie. 'I have indeed. Miss Fletcher and I are old friends. Though her skill as a speaker was something new to me. I'm deeply impressed.'

'Hello, Alec,' said Cassie quietly. 'I didn't see you in the audience.'

'I kept out of sight behind a pillar.' He pushed the book nearer. 'Please sign it for me—you're the first author I've actually met in the flesh.'

The emphasis he gave the last word brought the colour rushing to Cassie's cheeks and she bent hurriedly, scribbling 'To Alec Neville, with best wishes, Quinn Fletcher' on the flyleaf before handing the book to him with a polite social smile.

'I didn't expect to see you here tonight, Alec.'

'I'm here every night. It's my home for the moment, until my house is ready.' Mockery glinted in his eyes as he read the inscription on the book. As Ian Selby turned away to speak to someone else Alec leaned nearer. 'I thought you might have put love and kisses, Cassie, to an old friend like me.'

She gave him a kindling look as Ian Selby rejoined them to ask Cassie how she felt about an interview with the local radio station next day. She was quite happy to oblige, conscious of an inner glow of very human satisfaction that Alec was witness to her modest little triumph. After arrangements had been made for the interview Ian Selby offered Cassie a drink before she went home.

'Sorry to horn in, but I'm presuming on old acquaintance,' said Alec smoothly. 'Miss Fletcher and I were at Pennington General at the same time years ago. I'm sure you won't mind if I carry her off to the bar to catch up on old times.'

'Perhaps,' said Cassie with hard-won self-control, once they were seated at a secluded table in the bar, 'you should have asked *me* if I'd minded.'

'If I had you'd have said yes,' said Alec blandly, and ordered champagne.

Cassie stared at him impatiently. 'I can't drink champagne—I've got to drive home.'

'Champagne's obligatory for a celebration, and your performance tonight merits one, Cassie. You were damn good. Don't worry. I'll get you a taxi. You can pick up your car tomorrow when you come in to do this radio interview.' Alec lounged back in his chair, surveying her at length. 'So, Cassie. How does it feel to be a celebrity?'

'Since I'm only a very minor one, no different from usual,' she countered drily. 'Not that I object to the publicity if it sells more books.'

When the impressive bottle arrived in an ice-filled bucket Alec filled their glasses, held his up to her in toast, then said casually, 'It came as rather a surprise, by the way, to run into you at the theatre. You told me you never went out in the week.'

Cassie, expecting the question from the moment she'd set eyes on Alec, tasted her wine, unruffled. 'I should have said rarely rather than never. To be honest I'd forgotten I promised Liam I'd go to the theatre.'

'*Liam*?' Alec stared at her, frowning. 'Don't tell me that strapping young Adonis was your inspector, Cassie!'

'Oh, no,' she assured him airily. 'As happens all too often, Liam couldn't come at the last minute. Luckily my—my companion was quite happy to fill in.'

'Nice to have a second string so conveniently to hand,' said Alec caustically. 'I could see you were enjoying his company to the full in spite of the age-difference—or perhaps because of it!'

Cassie sipped her champagne, unmoved. 'I don't see why you're so annoyed, Alec. You weren't alone yourself.'

'My companion was Mrs Parkinson Mark Two,' he informed her tightly. 'Isobel was my hostess for the evening.'

Cassie hid a secret leap of pleasure at the information. 'Very striking woman.'

The bar was rapidly emptying. They were almost alone in their dimly lit corner as Alec eyed her with hostility. 'You obviously knew your companion very well.'

She nodded. 'Oh, yes. I go out with him a lot. I go out with Liam, too. Just as I used to spend quite a bit of time with one of my colleagues from the forensic lab, before he wanted to marry me, that was. Oh, and occasionally I go up to London to have lunch with my editor, who happens to be male and unattached. In short, Alec, no one has a monopoly on my time.'

'*Or* your bed?'

Cold, dark eyes stared stonily into hard, angry blue ones.

'I take exception to that,' said Cassie with deadly calm.

Alec breathed in deeply, swallowed the contents of his glass, then refilled it and topped up Cassie's. 'Sorry. That was uncalled for.'

Cassie, in the act of opening her mouth to explain about Ben, closed it again. If Ben was right Alec was jealous, and she found she rather fancied the idea of letting him fry. 'Apology accepted,' she said lightly, and looked at her watch. 'It's time I went home. Will you call this taxi you promised, please?'

Alec got up at once and went off to the public telephone in the foyer. When he got back Cassie was the sole occupant of the bar. He moved his chair closer to hers and sat down. 'There won't be one for a few minutes, I'm afraid, so we might as well finish off the champagne.'

'I should have abstained, and driven myself home.'

'Surely you'd have felt flat on your own after the euphoria of your success, Cassie?'

She looked at him sharply, but found no mockery in his intent blue eyes. 'I suppose I would,' she admitted, then shook her head as he made to refill her glass. 'No, thank you, Alec. I rarely drink very much at all. If I have any more I'll be telling you my life story again—whereas it's your turn to tell me yours.' She looked at him questioningly. 'Will you? We've got time to kill.'

Alec stared down into his glass. 'It's not something I generally talk about.'

'Then of course don't if you'd rather not,' she said at once.

'No. You satisfied my curiosity, it's only fair that I respond in kind.' He looked across at her, his face sombre. 'Life's strange, Cassie. When I accepted the job in Pennington I couldn't help wondering if I'd meet you again. But I was sure that even if I did you'd have married someone else years ago. I was convinced that was your reason for breaking up with me—that all the cloak-and-dagger stuff meant there was another man in your life somewhere.'

'As you made very clear at the time!' She raised an eyebrow. 'You know differently now.'

'So I do. But in London, during those first weeks after we parted, thoughts of you with some other man drove me insane—not during the day of course, I was too busy. But the nights—' His face darkened. 'I'm not saying I lived like a monk. I went out with any number of willing females in an effort to forget, and eventually, being human, and up to my eyes in work, I began to succeed. Then one day a girl was referred to me with a really bad, disfiguring scar on one side of her face. Before the car accident responsible for it she'd been a photographic model, and flawlessly beautiful.' Alec met Cassie's eyes squarely. 'I liked her. The accident put paid to her career but she was brave, trying hard to come to terms with it, and, to cap it all, from her good side she reminded me of you, Cassie.'

Alec had operated on Helen Fielding's face and the

end result had been very satisfactory. But her real scar was mental and went deep. Her lover, who'd been driving, had got off with only a few bruises, but ditched her after one look at her face in hospital.

'After she was discharged we began seeing each other socially,' said Alec, his face expressionless. 'I'd never let myself get involved with a patient before, but technically, of course, Helen was no longer a patient. She seemed so dependent on me—probably because I was the one who gave her back her looks.' He turned to look at Cassie. 'And from the first she made no secret of the fact that she found me physically attractive.'

Still raw and smarting from Cassie's treatment, Alec had reacted to Helen's overt adoration with the inevitable male response. Six months later they were married.

'So the no-strings Alec Neville, who blenched at any hint of commitment, promised to love, honour and cherish his bride until death did us part.' His mouth turned down bitterly. 'Lord, was I proud of myself! In the very act of speaking the vows I was thinking about you, Cassie. What I'd give to tell you how wrong you'd been about me.' He looked across at her still face suddenly. 'Not, you'll agree, the proper thoughts for a bridegroom.'

Cassie shook her head slowly, then pushed the champagne bucket towards him.

'No more for me, thanks.' He looked at her bleakly. 'Do you want the rest of the story?'

'Of course I do. Were you happy together?'

Alec thrust a hand over his thick, curly hair. 'Oddly enough, we were. Before the accident Helen had been the all-time party girl, but she took to domesticity with extraordinary zeal, learned to cook and worked hard at making the flat a home. It was a pleasure to return to it at night. And, no matter how late I was, Helen never nagged or complained. She was always eager to hear about my day in the theatre, what progress my patients had made. Our life together was good. Then one day—' Alec's mouth compressed. 'One day my list for the afternoon was postponed until the following morning, so I went home early. I surprised Helen with Barry Collins, the photographer and one-time lover who couldn't bear the sight of her ruined face. Now she was pretty again, he was back.'

'What did you do?'

Alec shrugged. 'Nothing. They weren't in bed together. They were merely drinking coffee and talking about old times. But Collins was very obviously having trouble keeping his hands off her. I suppose I should have been flattered. Helen's looks owed a lot to my skill.'

'How did Helen feel?'

'Guilty primarily.' His mouth twisted. 'I can still see the look of horror on her face when I walked in that day.'

'So what happened?' asked Cassie quietly.

'We had a hell of a row, needless to say. You, better than anyone, know what I'm like when I lose my temper. Helen admitted Collins had been round a few times before, but swore they'd only talked.' He shrugged. 'I didn't believe her, couldn't bring myself to touch her. I knew she was miserable, but I needed time to get over the fact that she'd been seeing Collins behind my back. Tragically, time wasn't something Helen had. Less than a week later she died.'

Cassie's eyes opened like saucers. 'Oh, Alec, no! How—?'

'Cerebral haemorrhage.'

'Were you with her?'

He nodded. 'I rushed her to the hospital but there was nothing anyone could do. Afterwards my guilt was the hardest part,' he said grimly.

Cassie leaned forward urgently. 'What guilt? You gave her back her looks and married her—what more could you have done?'

Alec met her eyes very squarely. 'I could have loved her.'

Cassie sat back in her seat, looking at his set, brooding face for a time. 'Alec,' she said at last, 'you did a lot for Helen—shared your life *and* your work with her. Most wives have to settle for a lot less than that, often before the honeymoon is over.'

'Would *you* settle for less?' he demanded.

Cassie shook her head. 'No, I wouldn't.'

'But you thought of sharing your home with someone at one time?'

She nodded, relieved to see the pain in his eyes

give way to something rather different. 'As I told you, it just wasn't on.'

'Why not?'

'He's too big.'

Alec's eyes narrowed. 'Then I take it you mean Mr Universe last night. Or do you have another outsize Romeo on a string?'

The mood underwent a lightning change. Cassie sat very straight in her chair, eyeing him militantly.

'I don't have anyone on a string.'

'Not even the good inspector?'

'Liam and I are just friends, Alec.'

'Not that old chestnut, Cassie!'

She glared at him. 'I met Liam when I was at the forensic lab, about the time I started to write. He agreed to help me in an advisory capacity, if you must know. From a research point of view he's been invaluable.'

'And from a more personal angle?'

She lifted her chin. 'That's my business.'

'How old is he?'

Cassie scowled. 'What's that got to do with anything?'

'It's to be hoped he's nearer your age than the young stud you were with last night.'

'Ugh!' Cassie ground her teeth in rage and would have leapt to her feet, but Alec leaned across the table and caught her hands in his, staring implacably into her eyes. 'Is he good, Cassie? Do you tremble for him the way you did for me the other night?'

'How dare you?' she said through her teeth.

A discreet cough from the barman brought them back to earth.

'Excuse me, Mr Neville. The taxi's come for Miss Fletcher.'

Alec rose to his feet with a word of thanks, ushering Cassie in front of him from the bar as though they'd been discussing nothing more emotive than the weather. Outside on the floodlit steps of the hotel Alec eyed the waiting taxi, then looked down at Cassie's stony face.

'Cassie, I didn't mean to sour the success of your evening.'

'You haven't,' she assured him with dignity. 'Thank you for the champagne.' She held out her hand formally, conscious of the curious eyes of the taxi driver. Alec took the hand in his, and held it.

'So, Cassie, we're all square. I know about you and you know about me. The salient points, at least.' He paused. 'Is that it? Do we now go our separate ways and forget we ever knew each other?'

'I don't think I'll ever quite be able to do that, Alec.' Cassie looked at him thoughtfully. 'If you give up making remarks like those back there I suppose there's no reason why we can't be friends.'

He smiled, the familiar mockery very much in evidence as he gave her back her hand. 'There's one very good reason, Cassie, as you know perfectly well.'

Cassie dismissed that impatiently. 'It's not an in-

surmountable barrier to friendship between two mature adults, surely, Alec.'

His eyes narrowed to gleaming slivers of conjecture. 'What do you have in mind?'

She shrugged. 'A meal now and then, perhaps.'
Cassie grinned suddenly. 'Or a trip to the theatre—
with each other this time. Maybe even the cinema.'

Alec's face lit up with the rare, sudden smile which
always changed him out of recognition. 'The last time
I went to the cinema, Cassie Fletcher, was with you!'

'You're having me on!' She shook her head at him
in amazement. 'High time you went again, then.'

'Done,' he said promptly. 'How about tomorrow?'

She shook her head. 'Sorry. But I could make it
Sunday—if you like.'

'I thought Sundays were out for you.'

'Not in the evenings.'

'Sunday it is, then. Will you meet me here, or shall
I come for you?'

Cassie thought for a moment. 'I'll come here, I
think.'

'Right. I'll give you dinner first.'

She shook her head. 'Sundays I eat at lunchtime.
I'll meet you in the bar about seven for a drink instead.' She looked towards the waiting car. 'I think
the driver's getting impatient. I must go, or I'll be
paying him a fortune.'

Alec walked down the steps with her and opened
the car door to settle her inside. 'Combe Aston,' he
told the driver, and handed him some money. 'That

should cover this and a return trip tomorrow. The lady needs to get back here in the afternoon.'

The driver nodded cheerfully. 'Right you are, guv, anything the lady wants.'

Cassie glowered at Alec for a moment, then smiled reluctantly. 'High-handed as ever. You haven't asked what film is on, by the way.'

'Whatever it is, I shan't have seen it,' he assured her, then stood back with a wave as the car moved off.

Liam called early next morning to apologise for his absence from her talk, said he'd heard it had gone well, and did she know that the Depardieu film she wanted to see was showing at the cinema?

'We could go to that Italian place afterwards,' he suggested.

Cassie did some rapid, guilty thinking. 'Oh, Liam, what a shame; I've just got to do some work this weekend for once. I've got a broadcast to record this morning for the local radio station, which means I must make up in the afternoon. I'll be staring at my screen for hours, so could I give my eyes a rest and just say yes to the meal?'

To her relief Liam, obviously with their recent differences uppermost in his mind, was only too ready to fall in with whatever Cassie wanted.

Unfortunately the work part of the programme was the last thing she wanted. She liked her Saturdays off. Now she'd be forced to stay at her machine all day after telling Liam she was going to, which meant she'd be tired and a bit short of her sparkling best in the evening.

Cassie rather enjoyed her radio interview. The presenter of the feature programme was warm with praise afterwards. Cassie, it seemed, unlike a great many people, hadn't been struck dumb or rendered too loquacious by the sight of a live microphone. Life, reflected Cassie, as she picked up her car at the Chesterton afterwards, was somewhat hectic of late. Ever since she'd met Alec again, if she pinned the change down to an actual date.

When Liam collected her in the evening he tried manfully to interest her in various subjects over dinner, but until he started talking about his work Cassie found it hard to respond. Once the subject of crime was established things were better, since Cassie was able to consult him about her new book, grateful when Liam provided some sound advice on one or two problems she'd been wrestling with during the day. Even so, she found she wasn't enjoying the evening as much as others spent in Liam's company. And his trained, probing mind had little trouble in detecting it.

Once the meal was over he began asking questions Cassie had no answer for, such as what was the matter, why had things begun to go so wrong between them lately, what could he do to put them right? When she failed to come up with anything satisfactory on any count Liam signalled abruptly for the bill, then ran with her through pouring rain to the car, asking her to go back to his place for a nightcap. He had a suggestion to make.

Cassie saw no reason why he couldn't make his suggestion back at Combe Cottage, where she would provide the nightcap without having to turn out again in the rain.

'You could stay the night with me,' he said, his lip jutting as he stared through the windscreen.

She eyed him in astonishment. He'd never asked that before. 'Was that the suggestion, Liam?'

'No, it bloody well wasn't,' he said explosively. 'It wasn't so much a suggestion as a proposal. I'm asking you to marry me, Cassie.'

Liam drove Cassie home, saw her to her gate in grim silence, then drove off the moment she was out of the car, not bothering to wait until she was safely inside. Cassie closed her door behind her with a heavy sigh and switched on every light, then made herself some tea, towelled her dripping hair and slumped on her sofa, utterly exhausted.

Her refusal had been very hard for Liam, she realised unhappily. He had never really recovered from his break up with Detta, which, she was convinced, was a major part of Liam's problem. Cassie's suggestion that he still loved his estranged wife had not gone down well at all. He'd flared up in a black rage new to their relationship, denied all feeling for Detta and tried to illustrate this by grabbing Cassie in an

embrace she objected to strongly, knowing it was fuelled more by anger than any real desire for her.

Such a shame, thought Cassie, depressed. If only
Liam had been content with friendship they could
have gone on seeing each other, which meant seeing
Kitty and Tess, too. Now that wasn't possible, and
she'd miss the twins.

Next day Cassie cooked lunch for Ben, who was
all ears as he heard the news.

'Mind you,' he said, as he helped himself to thirds
of roast beef, 'I couldn't quite see you and Liam as
a permanent arrangement, somehow. Never mind,
love, I'll set you up with someone at the firm.'

With dignity Cassie informed her brother that he
had no need to set her up with anyone.

'You'll miss going out with Liam, though,' said
Ben, beginning on glazed apple flan. 'Mmm, this is
good.'

'As it happens,' said Cassie airily, 'I have a date
this very evening, if that's what you youngsters still
call an appointment with the opposite sex.'

'Come off it, Grandma!' hooted Ben, flashing the
smile that mowed the majority of Cassie's sex down
like ninepins. He adopted a stern parental expression,
wagging his fork at her. 'And who may your follower
be, my dear? Will I approve?'

'He's male, unattached and solvent. What more do
you want?'

'It's what *you* want that we're discussing,
Catherine!'

Ben looked enquiring. 'Where's he taking you?'

'To the cinema,' said Cassie demurely.

'Am I allowed to ask who it is?'

'The man who was looking daggers at me at the theatre.' She grinned as Ben's dark eyebrows met his shock of flaxen hair. 'You were right. He got entirely the wrong impression, thinks you're a bit young for me.'

Ben tut-tutted. 'Surely you told him who I was!'

'No. I thought it rather fun to let him stew a bit.'

'This is all very sudden, isn't it?'

'Not really. I used to know him years ago, when I worked at the path lab. He was on the surgical staff at the General then.' Cassie explained Alec Neville's return to Pennington.

Ben eyed her, arrested. 'Cass—is he the one you were seeing when Mother was ill?'

Cassie looked back in surprise. 'I didn't think you'd remember.'

'I was twelve, not two! With enough marbles to know you were nuts over someone.' Ben gave her a very straight look. 'I remember what you were like when it was over, too. Did *he* break it off?'

'No. I did. He was going away to another job. Mother was so ill. What else could I do?'

'I see. But he's back now.' Ben traced patterns on the tablecloth with a fork. 'Does he want to take up where he left off?'

'I think so.'

'Do you?'

'I'm not sure.'

Ben got up to help clear away, unusually serious on the subject of second chances as he dried the dishes Cassie washed.

'Dad's to blame for your chronic cold feet where men are concerned, I suppose. Pity. I'd like to see you happy with someone, Cass,' he said gruffly.

'I don't have to have a man in tow to be happy, Ben! I've got my house, my garden and my writing. Even you, when your social calendar allows.' Cassie smiled cheerfully. 'Why should I ask for more?'

'Because, Cassie Fletcher, you'd make a fantastic wife and mother,' declared Ben.

Cassie gazed at him in surprise. 'But you disapprove of marriage!'

'For me, yes. But whatever guy you fancy had better have marriage in mind or I'll smash him to pulp,' said Ben casually, gave his astounded sister a hug and went off whistling to a session in his local gym.

CHAPTER SIX

WHEN Cassie arrived at the Chesterton later the evening was clear and beautiful, in sharp contrast to the night before. She'd chosen her clothes carefully: a beautifully cut cream wool skirt, scarlet wool blazer, red suede lace-up shoes and her hair left to hang loose from the combs catching it behind her ears. She felt a surge of gratification when she saw the look in Alec's eyes as he rose to greet her in the hotel's plush cocktail bar.

'Cassie, you look stunning,' he said, pulling out a chair for her.

After the trouble she'd taken Cassie was glad. 'Good. Could I have one of those non-alcoholic cocktails they do here?'

When their drinks were in front of them Cassie sipped appreciatively through a straw as Alec described a medical dinner he'd attended during the week.

'Though the speaker wasn't a patch on Miss Quinn Fletcher,' he informed her blandly, and smiled into her eyes. 'Either to listen to or to look at.'

Cassie gave him a suspicious look. 'Are you flirting with me, Alec?'

'Certainly not.' He raised a quizzical black eye-brow. 'Flirting's a bit dated, Cassie.'

She shrugged. 'I'm an old-fashioned girl.'

Alec smiled. 'Not a bit of it. You're the epitome of the self-sufficient female. Though I grant you've never been short of good old-fashioned principles!'

'Principles make poor companions sometimes.'

'Does that mean you get lonely now and then?'

Cassie thought about it. 'Not often. Usually I've got my fictional characters for company, Detective Sergeant Harriet Gale and the two men in her life.'

'Not to mention your good inspector,' he said shortly.

Cassie looked at him, noting absently that his jacket was made of such glove-soft leather it could almost have been velvet. A far cry from the leather biker's jacket of the old days. 'Liam proposed to me last night,' she said casually.

Alec frowned. 'Marriage?'

'Of course.'

'What answer did you give?'

'I suggested we just go on being friends.'

'How you do keep harping on the platonic, Cassie! What did the poor devil say to that?'

'Quite a lot.' Cassie pulled a face. 'Some of it was pretty unforgivable.'

'Rejection affects men that way,' Alec informed her affably. 'I seem to remember getting heated my-self in similar circumstances once upon a time.'

'But I wasn't sending Liam away!'

'If a man proposes marriage and gets offered friendship instead it's the next best thing, Cassie.'

'You sound sorry for him.'

'The hell I am!' Alec looked across at her. 'If you married your inspector he'd cross my name off your visiting list before you could sign yours on the register.'

She nodded. 'I wouldn't expect anything different. One man at a time, that's my motto.'

'Not so you'd notice. Lately you've been consorting with at least three of my sex, and that's only the ones I know about.'

'But I wasn't committed to any of you,' she pointed out. 'If I marry it will be different.'

'I should hope so,' he said, and stood up. 'Come on, or we'll be late. It's so long since I went to the cinema, I want my money's worth.'

The Cameo cinema was small, as its name implied, and by the time they arrived it was almost full. With no choice in the matter they found themselves shown to a pair of end seats against the wall near the back. The moment the lights went down Alec took her hand in his and sat as close as physically possible, which meant that from start to finish of *Jean de Florette* Cassie had problems in following the subtitles. All her concentration was centred on the grasp of Alec's fingers, the warmth from his long, elegant frame fuelling her own body heat to the point where she found it hard to breathe.

When they emerged into the starlit night afterwards

Cassie was glad of the concealing darkness, sure her cheeks matched her blazer as they walked back through the quiet town to the Chesterton.

'Did you enjoy the film?' asked Alec.

'Very much.'

'I might have, too, in other circumstances. As it was, I found it hard to concentrate,' he said wryly. 'Pity I let you drive in tonight. Now I can't even take you home.'

'You didn't *let* me drive in, Alec,' she said tartly. 'I arranged it that way purposely.'

Alec gave her a long, arctic look as they reached her car. 'Were you afraid that if I drove you home I'd carry you over your threshold and demand your body in return for a cinema ticket?'

'No, of course not,' she retorted.

'Cassie, it was you who proposed we get together now and then. But frankly, if you panic about my leaping on you every time we do it just isn't worth it.' He tipped a hard, urgent finger under her chin. 'One thing I would say before you run home to your doll's house: This isn't a dress rehearsal. It's life. You should live some of it—time's ticking by.' He held the door open for her and Cassie got in, closed it firmly behind her then wound down the window.

'I'm quite happy to spend time with you, Alec,' she said evenly, 'as long as you understand there's no question of spending any of it in bed.'

Alec frowned blackly. 'Is that an ultimatum, Cassie?'

'I prefer to call it being straight with you.'

He gazed down at her, his eyes inscrutable in the light from the street-lamps. 'Then I'll be straight with you,' he said very distinctly. 'Ultimatums of that kind, even from you, Cassie, are neither to my taste nor are they in the least bit necessary. A pity. The gap between us is obviously too wide to bridge after all this time.'

Cassie stared at him blankly, but there was no mistaking his meaning. This time the rejection was coming from him. She gave an angry little shrug. 'Then there's no more to be said. Goodnight, Alec.' She switched on the ignition, and to her utter dismay Alec Neville stepped back and let her drive away.

Cassie stormed into Combe Cottage in a foul mood. She stamped upstairs and threw her blazer on a chair, then, mindful of its newness and cost, she hung it up with the rest of her clothes and went to stand under a shower. By the time she emerged, wet and shivering, her temper had cooled down, leaving her flat and miserable and very much aware that she'd cut off her nose to spite her face. You're getting a bit above yourself, Cassie Fletcher, she told her reflection as she dried her hair. Turning Liam down last night, laying down the law with Alec tonight. A couple of days ago there'd been three men in her life. Now she was down to one. And he was her brother.

Cassie propped herself up in bed with a book, but read the same page over and over without taking in a word before finally tossing the book away in disgust. Her alarm clock ticked loudly alongside her, measuring out her life in a way she'd never noticed before. She glared at it, then her eyes narrowed. It was still only a little past eleven. Without giving herself time to think, she reached for the phone and rang the Chesterton. She asked to be put through to Mr Alec Neville's room then waited what seemed like forever before the familiar voice barked, 'Neville,' on the other end.

'It's Cassie,' she said rapidly. 'Will you come and have dinner with me here on Wednesday?'

There was a prolonged pause. 'Why?'

Another silence, this time on Cassie's part. 'While I was driving home I had time to think. I realised there was no need for me to—to talk conditions where you're concerned.'

'You mean that I might actually be civilised enough to recognise a "no" if I heard it?' he enquired caustically.

Bitterly regretting her impulse, Cassie forced herself to keep calm. 'All right, Alec. Forget it. Sorry I disturbed you.'

'Don't ring off!' he said abruptly. 'What time shall I come?'

Cassie took a deep breath, dismayed to find she was trembling. 'Eightish?'

'Fine.'

'Right. I—I'll expect you then.'

Cassie rang off and lay with her arm across her eyes, heart beating like a bass drum. Now, of course,

Alec was bound to think that the invitation was to a great deal more than a meal. Nor could she blame him. But under the shower she'd had a sudden vivid picture of pouring rain on a day ten years ago, and Alec storming away from her along the riverbank after she'd ended it between them. Now, by some strange quirk of fate, he was back in her life, and she was still saying no, and for the life of her she couldn't think why.

She heaved a great sigh, hugging a pillow to her chest. Her life had been so cosy and well-ordered up until a few weeks ago. Then one astonished look at Alec across his desk and her world was a different place entirely, with uncharted seas and areas labelled 'here be dragons'. Cassie hurled the pillow away and went downstairs to make herself some tea, then returned to bed with her mug and thought long and hard while she drank. The physical attraction between herself and Alec was as strong as ever, she conceded. No one since had roused anything like the response she felt to his merest touch. But Cassie at twenty had been madly in love with Alec Neville. Cassie at thirty-something was a very different proposition. It was useless to pretend she was indifferent to him, or he to her. But whether it had anything to do with love on either side was open to question.

Love? Cassie's eyes narrowed. Was that what she really wanted? Love usually meant marriage, or at the very least some kind of partnership. But when Liam had proposed marriage she'd recoiled as though he'd suggested committing a crime. But would the recoil be the same if the proposal came from Alec? She grinned suddenly. All Alec wanted was to spend time with her, not marry her! He was probably off marriage for good after his first experience of it. While Cassie Fletcher had her life sorted out exactly as she wanted it, with a home she loved and career which earned her enough to keep herself in reasonable comfort in it. So Alec was coming to dinner again—it was no big deal. If he misunderstood the reason behind her invitation there'd be no problem. He was the one who said he recognised a 'no'. On which comforting thought Cassie switched off her light and slid down in the bed and left all further conjecture for the morning.

After her extra day's work the previous Saturday Cassie was well ahead of schedule on her book, and on the morning Alec was due she felt fully entitled to take an hour off to pay a visit to the village shop. This was a surprisingly well-stocked establishment, one of a fast vanishing breed, and Cassie, along with most people in Combe Aston, patronised the shop regularly, preferring friendly, personalised service to the lower prices of Pennington supermarkets.

Wednesday was a bright autumn day, redolent with the scent of woodsmoke as Cassie bumped her way up the lane on her mountain bike before reaching the smoother ride into the village itself. The journey was a mile door to door, which ruled out shopping in any great quantity, but Cassie had long since worked out how much she could carry home at a time, liked the exercise, and only resorted to her car when the weather was bad. In the shop she chatted with some neighbours who'd heard her broadcast, and when she'd made her purchases asked the Bowyers, the friendly couple who ran the shop, to cancel her papers for the period two weeks away when she was due to visit her mother in Wales. Afterwards she cycled home with her basket of goodies at a brisk pace, her mind occupied, as usual, with the complexities of her current plot.

Cassie put her shopping away, made a pot of coffee, and settled down to work on her book, which had reached the stage where elegant, saturnine Rufus Cairns, pathologist, and attractive, feisty Detective Sergeant Harriet Gale were poring over the pathology report on the pretty victim of a particularly brutal murder. Her appetite diminished by the details, along with a nervous excitement she couldn't quite suppress, Cassie skipped lunch, and worked through until it was time to think about the meal, which she'd purposely kept very simple to avoid any misleading overtones of festivity.

When Alec arrived Cassie was curled up on the sofa in an oversized clover-pink sweater and old jeans tight from recent washing, nibbling from a plate of peanuts as she watched the end of the television soap she was addicted to.

'Come in,' she called when he rang. 'The door's open.'

Alec strode into the room, his face like thunder as she scrambled to her feet to greet him. 'Cassie, are you mad? You shouldn't leave your door unlocked— I could have been anyone.'

'But I was expecting you.' Her eyes widened as she took in his formal chalk-striped suit. 'Gosh, you look very grand.'

'Sorry, no time to change. I've come straight from St John's. There was a mix-up on my list and one of my patients came an hour late.' Alec's hard blue eyes softened as he took in her casual clothes and lack of make-up. 'You look very young dressed like that, Cassie. Takes me back in time just to look at you.'

Which wasn't at all the effect she'd aimed for.

'Would you like to take your jacket off?' she suggested briskly. 'The contrast won't be so marked.'

Alec dispensed with his jacket and removed his tie, rotating his head on his neck wearily. 'This is just what I need,' he said with a sigh, as without asking Cassie thrust a glass of beer in his hand and waved him to a chair. He let himself down and stretched out his long legs, eyeing her as she switched off the television in favour of her CD player. 'So how are things with you, Cassie? Is the muse functioning?'

She shrugged as she offered him some salted nuts. 'I had a sticky patch early this afternoon, but I worked my way out it. Tomorrow I'll see if I got it right. How was your day?'

'Hectic. I was operating right up to the first appointment on my private list.' He smiled. 'So whatever smells so good out there I hope you made a lot of it. I'm starving.'

'I always make a lot.'

'Ah, yes. The formidable young man at the theatre. He must take some fuelling.'

Cassie nodded, unruffled. 'He does. But actually I often make more than I need and reheat it next day to save myself trouble when I'm working. It's a bit of an effort to cook for just one some nights.'

Alec dispatched some of his drink, his eyes expressionless as he looked at her in silence for a while. 'You once told me you never socialised in the week, so one way and another your invitation came as something of a surprise,' he remarked at last.

'I imagine it did,' she agreed, and looked at him very squarely. 'On the way home on Sunday I felt a bit silly, to be honest, about laying down the law and so on. Afterwards I kept thinking of your remark about dress rehearsals, so I swallowed my pride and rang you.'

'I'm glad you did.' Alec slid deeper into the chair, his eyes warmer. 'So no more talk about rules and regulations. As you so rightly say, it was never in the least necessary, Cassie.'

She looked at him for a long, considering moment, then nodded. 'Right. And I made it mid-week,' she added, 'because I worked last Saturday, which meant I could spare some time today to prepare a meal.'

'I thought Saturday was your day off.'

Cassie explained about Liam's plan to see *Jean de Florette* on the Saturday night, and how she'd made the excuse of staring at her screen all day to get out of it. 'So, having said I intended to work, I worked,' she finished sheepishly, flushing at the look on his face.

'Couldn't you have just told him you were seeing the film the following night with me?'

'I wish I had now,' she said glumly. 'The net result could hardly have been more final.'

'Poor devil.'

'Poor me, too! Liam's been a great help in the past with research for my books. I can't expect that any more.' She glanced at her watch. 'Time I threw some pasta in a pot. It's nothing special tonight, by the way.'

'Don't worry, Cassie, message received—loud and clear.' His eyes gleamed with mockery as she went past, chin in the air, on her way to the kitchen.

Later Alec ate with fastidious, complimentary greed when confronted with pasta in mushroom and tomato sauce served with a salad of avocado, spinach and crisp grilled bacon.

'That was a vast improvement on a meal in my room at the Chesterton,' he said with a sigh as Cassie put a large slab of Single Gloucester cheese in front of him afterwards. 'I couldn't have faced the dining-room tonight.'

'When will you move into the house?'

'If all goes to plan fairly soon.' He eyed her challengingly. 'How about giving me a hand on moving day? No muscles required, I promise, but a feminine eye would be useful when it comes to hanging pictures and so on.'

'If I'm back from Wales in time I'd love to, Alec.'

'Wales?'

She nodded. 'I'm off to stay with Mother and Mike in a couple of weeks.'

'Is this a sudden decision?'

'No. I usually go there once I've finished a book, but last time I had my hand done. I brought maternal wrath down on my head by keeping quiet about it until the hand was in use again, so I'm taking time off from the grind for a little break now instead. I suffer withdrawal symptoms if I don't see my mother fairly regularly.'

'You're obviously very close to her.'

Cassie nodded. 'For more than the usual mother-daughter reasons, as you already know.'

'You must have been shattered when she was so ill. I just wish I'd known at the time,' said Alec soberly.

'If she'd been a little *less* ill perhaps I would have told you. As it was—' Cassie shrugged. 'Anyway, let's not refine over things past. Tell me what you've been doing today.'

The evening progressed very pleasantly. In the old days their rapport had been as much mental as physical, and in this respect nothing had changed. Cassie was so deeply interested in Alec's work, and he in hers, that all too soon it was midnight and Alec got up to go.

Cassie walked with him down the garden path to the gate, where he paused, taking her hand in his.

'Thank you, Cassie. For the talk as well as the meal. It was just what I needed.'

'Good.' She looked at him steadily. 'It was the same for me.'

Alec's hand tightened on hers as he bent to kiss her cheek. 'I'm glad. I'll ring you. Goodnight.'

Cassie went back into the house in pensive mood. Alec, she knew perfectly well, had been showing her that he was perfectly happy to spend the evening deep in conversation. Which was what she'd been rabbiting on about on Sunday evening, of course. So why wasn't she more cheerful? Because, Catherine Fletcher, she informed herself as she washed up, you want conversation *and* kisses, the latter a trifle more impassioned than the chaste variety Alec bestowed on you just now.

True to his word, Alec rang the following evening to thank her for dinner, and ask for her company another evening. Saturday was out for him, he told her with regret, but apart from his rounds on Sunday morning the rest of the day was his own after all.

'Come for a run in the country, Cassie. Afterwards I'll give you a tour of the house in Beaufort Square, then dinner somewhere. I'll pick you up.'

Cassie smiled to herself. Alec was obviously proceeding with care. But unless ten years had effected a remarkable character change it was probably quite an effort for him—hence the ineluctable hint of command in his invitation. 'I'd like that very much. But I can't say when to the minute I can make it, so I'll save you the trip and meet you at the hotel early afternoon some time. I'll ring you from Reception when I arrive.'

With admirable forbearance Alec refrained from asking her why she couldn't come earlier, and went on chattering a few minutes longer before he said goodnight.

Ben objected strongly when he learned Cassie had put off meeting Alec earlier just to give her brother lunch.

'I don't have to come every Sunday!' He gave her a cocky grin. 'I'm sure I could get some other lady to feed me if I asked nicely.'

'I'm sure you could, too,' retorted Cassie. 'And you'll have to next week when I go off to Wales. Besides, an hour can't make much difference to Alec.'

'Cass, take my advice. I only got a quick look at this man of yours at the theatre, but from where I was standing he didn't seem the type you could mess about much.'

'I am not messing him about,' she said crossly. 'I just thought I'd feed you first, before I went out with him, more fool me. I wish I hadn't bothered now.'

'Temper, temper!' Ben eyed her closely. 'You look tired. Burning the midnight oil?'

'No, but I worked yesterday again, so that I can enjoy my holiday in Wales with a clear conscience.' She eyed him doubtfully. 'Do I look so haggish, then?'

Ben surveyed his sister's oval brown eyes and unruly curls judiciously, swept a look over her chocolate-brown jersey and faded coral-pink denims and shook his head. 'Considering your age, you're in pretty good nick.'

'Thanks a bunch.'

'Want a lift into town?'

'No fear. Your driving puts years on me—years I can't afford, apparently, brother dear!'

If Cassie had been harbouring any doubts about her state of preservation they were scotched the moment she met Alec, who was gratifyingly complimentary about her appearance. She'd added the coral jacket that matched up with her denims, brown leather boots, and tied up her hair with a white silk scarf printed with pomegranates.

'You look about sixteen in that get-up,' he informed her as he helped her into his car.

'I do hope you mean that,' she said with feeling. 'Sometimes it takes fortitude to face myself in the mirror in the morning.'

'Nonsense. You looked older when you were twenty.'

'I was such a sobersides, wasn't I?' she agreed, able to laugh about it now. 'Twenty going on forty!'

Alec, who was wearing an impressive leather jacket with a dark blue sweater and silvery moleskin trousers, chuckled as he made for the hilly countryside north of Pennington. The afternoon was still, with hazy sunshine and a very autumnal feel about it, and Cassie slid lower in her seat, feeling more relaxed and happy than she had for a long time as they talked with the ease of old friends, no hint of sexual tension in the air as Alec drove through several photogenic Cotswold villages until he found one with a tea-shop offering crumpets and toasted teacakes to visitors.

Afterwards they returned to Pennington and made for Beaufort Square. Cassie was very impressed by the early-nineteenth-century house Alec had chosen for his home. It was on three floors, with lots of space, high ceilings and moulded cornices, the ground floor reserved for consulting-rooms.

'Living quarters on the first floor,' said Alec, and led her up the uncarpeted stairs to a large, inviting room with a peaceful view of the sizeable back garden.

'That'll take some looking after,' commented Cassie, peering down at it.

'I'll have to get someone in,' he agreed, and went on through two other rooms and a kitchen, then up a second flight of stairs to a pair of bedrooms on the top floor, both of them large, with adjoining bathrooms.

'A lot of house for one man,' said Cassie doubtfully. 'Couldn't you have found something more compact?'

'I liked this one. You obviously don't share my enthusiasm,' he said drily.

'Of course I do. It's beautiful,' she said at once. 'I suppose I'm used to my doll's house in Combe Aston. But there's a wonderfully serene atmosphere here. I felt it the moment I came through the door.'

'So did I.' Alec smiled down at her. 'It seems we still tune in to each other's wavelength, Cassie, ten-year gap or not.'

She smiled back uncertainly. 'Yes—yes, I suppose we do.'

He took her hand. 'Come on, give me the benefit of your advice. The office downstairs is full of carpet samples. Tell me which you like best.'

CHAPTER SEVEN

CASSIE'S life moved into a new phase, with Alec's regular presence a stimulating adjunct to it. Afraid at first that this would undermine her concentration on her work, she found it had quite the reverse effect. She opened her eyes on the world each day with an enthusiasm which quite revitalised her writing. Even to her own critical eyes she could see that the work done lately was of a high standard. There was an underlying excitement in it that reflected her own mood and provided a fillip to the triangular relationship between her heroine, Harriet Gale, her dour but attractive boss, Inspector James Fraser, and Rufus Cairns, the pathologist Harriet grew more and more involved with in each of the thrillers Cassie wrote.

'I shall miss you when you're in Wales,' said Alec moodily as he drove her home one night.

Cassie smiled unseen in the darkness, pleased by his admission. 'I promise I'll get back in good time to give you a hand when you move in.'

'Must you insist on driving?' he said disapprovingly. 'Changing gear for hours with that hand won't improve it. Unless you're not going alone, of course.'

'I'm going to stay with my *mother*,' she reminded him.

'For all I know your mother might approve of your strapping young Adonis.'

'Very true,' said Cassie with a grin, and turned to him as he killed the engine at her gate. 'Alec, look, it's time I explained about him—'

'Don't! I don't want to hear,' said Alec roughly, and pulled her into his arms to stop her mouth with kisses which drove all thoughts of anyone else clean out of her head. 'You notice I'm restricting this intoxicating pastime to the car,' he said huskily, and kissed her again at length. 'Otherwise,' he said against her mouth, 'you'd think I was demanding access to your bed.'

'I wasn't thinking at all,' she whispered, and kissed him back with such uninhibited fervour that both of them were shaken when they separated a second time.

Alec stared down into her eyes, breathing raggedly. 'And now, I suppose, you're going to run up your path and lock yourself in your little castle, while I go back to my empty hotel room and take a cold shower. Cassie, I can't take much more of this.'

Cassie closed her eyes and rubbed her cheek against his. 'By the time I get back, absence may have fulfilled its usual function.'

'Unnecessary where I'm concerned,' he assured her, in command of himself with unflattering speed. 'Don't worry. I'm not suggesting I come in for so-called coffee. Ring me the minute you get back from Wales, Cassie.'

'I'll ring you *from* Wales if you like.'

'Do that. But I won't be back from this trip to London until mid-week. A pity you're not leaving tomorrow, when I do.'

'I know. But I've got a reporter coming round in the afternoon, remember, complete with photographer to do a piece on me for the *Pennington Weekly Herald*. Seems I'm flavour of the month lately.' Cassie thrust her hands through her loosened hair, smiling at him. 'Shall I leave my hair down like this? Or is it too frivolous for a crime writer?'

Alec pulled her close again and kissed her hard, then pushed her away, scowling. 'Scrape it back in a bun and try to look ugly, Cassie. I object to the idea of every Tom, Dick and Harry with the price of a newspaper able to drool over you.'

She stared at him in astonishment. 'Are you serious?'

'Too right I am.' He smiled suddenly. 'Bloody immature for my advanced years, I grant you, but where you're concerned I tend to regress ten years at the drop of a hat.'

Cassie gave him a delighted smile. 'Make sure you buy a *Herald*, just the same. Goodnight, Alec. Take care in the big city.'

'You do the same in Wales. *Bon voyage*, Cassie.'

Much to her mother's amusement Cassie became visibly restless after only a few days in the pretty stone house Kate and Mike had bought in Wales. Bryn Morfa stood in a niche in a hillside looking down on the sweep of Cardigan Bay, and normally Cassie loved it. In summer when the sun shone she lazed on the terrace Mike had constructed, ate her mother's simple, perfectly cooked meals and thoroughly enjoyed the pampering administered by the other two.

This time it was different. Winter was almost at hand, the weather was cold and blustery, and Cassie missed Alec more than she would have believed possible. To counteract this she took Kate on shopping expeditions to Cardigan, walked miles with Taff, the shaggy black and white mongrel, played board games in the evenings or dragged the other two away from their log fire to the local pub after dinner.

In the end Kate couldn't stand it any longer and demanded an explanation. And once she started on the subject Cassie couldn't stop talking. Mike was called in to listen as the whole story came out, not only about Alec's reappearance in her life, but the details of the prologue to it, ten years earlier.

Mike, understanding at last why his clever, attractive stepdaughter fought shy of lasting relationships with any of her men friends, was blunt with his advice. If this man was the one to make her happy then she should get herself back home and tell him so. Kate was in full agreement.

Cassie took their advice and drove home next day. A phone call to the Chesterton before she left confirmed that Mr Neville was still away, much to her disappointment. She left a message to say she would be home that evening, then set off on the long cross-country journey, obliged to prolong it by a detour to Ben's flat before going home, to deliver a large fruit cake her mother had made for him. Cassie caught him in for once, just as he was ordering a take-away from the local Thai restaurant. He promptly doubled the order, gave her a welcoming bearhug and assured her he wasn't going out until later.

He frowned suddenly. 'Though, now I come to think of it, I wasn't expecting you back until next week. Mother throw you out?'

'Of course not—I just wanted to get back to work.'

'Pull the other one, Cass! Panting to get back to your consultant more like it.'

Rather to her brother's surprise Cassie didn't bother to deny it. She reported on her stay in Wales instead, passed on various maternal messages over the meal, received a progress report from Ben on his job and his love life, and was about to leave for home, when Ben suddenly produced two copies of the *Weekly Herald*.

'I almost forgot,' he crowed, and turned pages until he found a picture of Cassie looking remarkably severe on her sofa, with two smaller photographs below it, one of her study, with her award and her books in prominence, the other of her sitting-room.

'WHO SAYS CRIME DOESN'T PAY?' was the headline. The article went on to describe the young, attractive crime writer at home, enjoying the rewards of her labours at her idyllic cottage in the Cotswolds.

Cassie wrinkled her nose. 'Tone's a bit lurid—I don't like the photograph, either.'

'Who would?' agreed Ben. 'Why are you rigged out like Whistler's mother on an off-day?'

Cassie grinned. 'I had my reasons. Though I'm sorry now. What a fright! Do you think anyone will ever buy my books again?'

Although it was still relatively early when Cassie finally arrived home she was more than ready for bed. She garaged the car, took out her suitcase, hefted the box of provisions provided by her mother and went wearily up the path to the cottage, eager for a hot bath and a good sleep. She unlocked the front door, dumped her suitcase in the tiny hall and turned on the lights as she went into the sitting-room. She stopped dead in the doorway, her tired yawn changing to a screech of horror.

The room was in chaos, the chintz-covered cushions from the sofa in a pile on the floor with the books from the shelves hurled anyhow on top. Everything else remotely portable seemed to be missing. Cassie stood transfixed, her eyes like saucers above the box of food she was clutching to her chest. The cabinet with the compact disc player, the speakers that went with it, the Pembroke table, a pair of much loved Meissen figurines left her by her grandmother, television, video recorder, pictures—everything was gone.

Cassie's heart gave a sudden, sickening thump. The burglar could still be in the house! She went quietly into the kitchen and turned the light on with one hand, the other clutching the box of groceries to her chest like a shield, but the only evidence of an intruder was a neat hole in the glass panel in the outer door. Cassie stared at it, teeth chattering, then put the box down and tiptoed back through the house to creep upstairs, reminding herself that Detective Sergeant Harriet Gale wouldn't have thought twice about confronting an intruder.

To her great relief Cassie's courage wasn't put to the test. No one was lurking behind a bedroom door, poised for attack. Her empty jewellery box lay on top of the bedclothes dumped on the floor, her mattress was heaved to one side, her dressing-table drawers were all wrenched from their moorings, and even the pine cabinet in the bathroom was open, with its contents littered over the floor. Only the spare bedroom, which had nothing to offer other than a bed and a couple of chairs, was in anything like a reasonable state. Her fright replaced by sudden, burning fury, Cassie raced downstairs to her office to ring the police and found her mobile phone had vanished too. Worse still, so had her word processor. Cassie flew to her filing cabinet, her hands shaking as she took out the metal box used to store her disks. They, at least, were still there; complete with her half-written story on one of them. Her breath left her in a great swoosh of relief as she sat down with a bump on her swivel chair.

But after a moment or two she jumped to her feet purposefully. Wailing and gnashing of teeth would get her nowhere. First she'd call the police, then, since Alec was still away, she'd ring Ben. Her brother's large presence was infinitely to be desired in the present circumstances. On the kitchen telephone she informed the police of the break-in, but the only response from Ben was on his answering machine. While she was leaving a message to tell him what had happened it dawned on her that her microwave was another absentee; as was the toaster, her transistor radio and, the last straw, her electric kettle. Cassie slammed the phone down, incensed. She wanted hot, strong tea at the moment more than anything in the world. Without much hope she opened the kitchen cupboards, then sighed with relief at the sight of pots and pans. The burglar hadn't been interested in non-electrical appliances. Good thing the cooker was a fixture, she thought grimly.

Cassie put a pan of water on to boil, then stowed the groceries away, beginning to shiver uncontrollably with reaction. She took a sweater from her suitcase and put a teabag in a mug, but long before the pan of water boiled she heard a car outside, followed by a loud tattoo on her front door. Deeply impressed by police promptitude, Cassie ran to open it, her eyes wide with astonishment as instead of a uniform she saw an elegant dark suit topped by the lean, smiling face of Alec Neville.

'I got your message, so I decided to take a chance and come straight to see you,' he informed her, looking pleased with himself.

Cassie suddenly went to pieces. She threw herself into his arms and hugged him convulsively, sobbing so incoherently that Alec picked her up bodily in alarm. He held her close, making soothing noises as he nudged the door shut behind him and carried her into the sitting-room, then almost dropped her at the sight which greeted him. 'What the—? Cassie, what the hell happened? Are you hurt?' He set her on her feet with a bump and turned her face up to his with an ungentle hand. 'Were you attacked? Assaulted? Tell me!'

Cassie shook her head, sniffing inelegantly as she knuckled the tears away. 'No. Nothing like that. I— I wasn't here. I walked in on this mess when I arrived back.' She bit her trembling lip. 'Oh, Alec, they took my grandmother's Meissen figurines, my word processor—even the *kettle*!'

Alec's lips twitched involuntarily at the last before he pulled her close, his cheek on her hair. 'Never mind that. They're just things—replaceable things, Cassie. You are not.' He held her in his arms for some time, until her sobs died away and her shivering diminished enough to satisfy him that she was calmer.

'Right,' he said at last, putting her away from him gently. 'Better? Have you got any brandy?'

'I don't know what I've got—I haven't looked properly. The police want to see it as it is.'

'Ah, yes, the police.' Alec led her into the kitchen and sat her down at the table. 'Does this mean your inspector will come galloping hotfoot to your rescue?'

'I doubt it,' she said miserably. 'A bit below his touch, I should think.'

The police, complete with scene-of-crime officer, arrived in due course, and thorough forensic tests were carried out throughout the house. They made as complete an inventory of the missing articles as they could in the circumstances, since Cassie's brain wasn't functioning with enough of its usual efficiency to be sure she hadn't overlooked something. Fortunately Mike had insisted on marking all her possessions in ink visible only under ultra-violet light. This won praise from the sergeant, though he was strongly disapproving when he heard Cassie hadn't thought to inform the police that she was going away. He'd seen her picture in the paper, he informed her, and in his opinion it was probable the burglar had done the same, fancying his chance after seeing her possessions in plain view in the photograph.

After the police had gone Alec replaced the cushions on the living-room sofa and insisted Cassie lie down while he went to the kitchen to make the tea she still yearned for. She put her feet up obediently, then jumped out of her skin as the front door burst open and Ben hurtled into the room, his eyes blazing in his pale face under the shock of bright hair. He grabbed Cassie up into his arms and nearly crushed the life out of her as he rapped out much the same questions Alec had earlier.

'They didn't hurt you, love?' he asked urgently. 'I mean—'

'No, no,' she assured him breathlessly. 'I found it like this. The police think it happened nights ago.'

Ben gave a great sigh of relief, cast an eye round the room and hugged her close again. 'You can't stay here tonight. I'll take you back to my place.' Suddenly he released Cassie so abruptly that she nearly fell over. He flushed slightly as he met the eyes of the man surveying them coldly from the kitchen doorway.

'Sorry!' said Ben, embarrassed. 'Didn't know you had company, Cass.'

'I was just leaving,' said Alec curtly. 'Since you're obviously in such good hands, Cassie, I'll be on my way—'

'Let me introduce you first,' she interrupted. 'Alec, this is Ben, my baby brother. Ben, meet Alec Neville, the new consultant plastic surgeon at the General.'

Alec stared from one to the other, gave Cassie a narrowed, kindling look, then held out his hand to Ben. 'How do you do?'

'Glad to meet you,' returned Ben, then scowled blackly at Cassie. 'You mean you still hadn't told him about me? Am I the skeleton in the cupboard or something?'

Alec's lips twitched. 'A rather substantial skeleton! Cassie somehow forgot to mention you were her brother. I thought your relationship with her was a trifle—different.'

Ben grinned widely. 'Her bit of fluff, you mean? Anyway, now you know I'm nothing of the sort, don't *you* think Cass should come home with me—at least for tonight?'

'It's what I think that matters,' his sister said crossly, before Alec could say a word. 'I'm staying put, thank you just the same. This is my home and nothing and no one's going to frighten me out of it.'

'Are you sure, Cassie?' said Alec, frowning. 'Why not do as Ben says and come back tomorrow to clear up?'

Cassie shook her head. 'No. I'll be fine.'

Ben shrugged philosophically. 'OK, then, if that's how you want it. I'd better be off. I'll give you a ring tomorrow, Cass.'

'Right.' She smiled at him reassuringly. 'Don't worry—and if you speak to Mother don't mention any of this. No need to upset her. There's nothing she can do.'

She saw her brother to the door, then went back into the sitting-room, quailing secretly at the look on Alec's face.

'So the young Adonis is your brother after all, Cassie Fletcher,' he said grimly. 'Was it fun, making me jealous?'

She met the steely blue eyes defiantly. 'Yes. In the beginning. Then I tried to tell you who he was the night before you left, but you said you didn't want to hear.'

'For obvious reasons. I resented the boy's physical attributes.' Alec examined her face, shaking his head. 'It never occurred to me you were related. Apart from the eyes there's no resemblance at all. Young Ben is most people's idea of your average Greek god.'

'Thanks a lot,' she snapped, glaring. 'Now if you've finished with the pleasantries I'll say good-night. If I don't start clearing up soon I'll never get to bed.'

Alec shook his head and closed the space between them to take her stiff, resentful body in his arms. 'I'm staying. Otherwise I'd have insisted you went home with Ben.'

Cassie wrenched free indignantly. 'You can't *insist* I do anything, Alec Neville!'

'True,' he said, unmoved, and shrugged off his jacket. 'Nevertheless, if you won't move elsewhere I shall just stay here tonight. Don't worry, I'll sleep on the sofa. I'll rest a damn sight easier on that than I would at the Chesterton, worrying about you.'

Cassie let out a shaky sigh. 'Then in that case thank you, Alec. To be honest I wasn't really looking for-ward to being on my own tonight. This business has knocked me off balance a bit.'

'As well it might,' he said, eyeing the chaotic room. 'Now, first things first. Would you happen to own anything as practical as a hammer and nails and a piece of wood big enough to do something about that kitchen door?'

Combe Cottage proved so sadly lacking in any aids to carpentry that in the end Alec enlisted Cassie's help in heaving her grandmother's Welsh dresser across the broken door as a gesture towards security. Afterwards they restored the sitting-room to as near normality as possible in its denuded state, then went upstairs to tackle Cassie's bedroom.

Cassie shuddered at the sight of it, then gathered up all her underwear and made it into a bundle with the linen from the bed.

'The thought of anyone pawing through my things makes me feel grubby,' she said in angry distaste, and took everything downstairs to thrust it in the washing machine.

By the time she got back Alec had returned the drawers and the mattress to their normal places, rescued the overturned bedside lamp and gathered up the empty jewel case along with shards of china from an ornament broken in the course of the robbery. While Cassie saw to her bed Alec went into the bathroom and restored the contents of the pine cupboard to their rightful places.

'I'm glad I didn't do this before I met Ben,' he said with a grin, when Cassie joined him. 'Finding a razor and aftershave among the toothpaste and aspirin would have had me thinking the worst.'

'Ben stays the night sometimes,' said Cassie, yawning. 'He was the one who shared with me for a bit until he found a place of his own, but Combe Cottage is the last place for someone of Ben's dimensions.' She sighed. 'Right. I'll just strip the bed in the spare room and put clean sheets on it and that's it, I think.'

Alec touched a hand to her hair. 'You look shattered, Cassie.'

She frowned. 'You'll be the same, if you've got a long list tomorrow.'

'I haven't. I wasn't sure if I'd get back today, so I kept tomorrow free.' He paused at the head of the stairs. 'I fancy a Scotch—I noticed they kindly left some behind. How about you?'

'Could you possibly make me some more tea?'

He laughed. 'I don't pretend to be a very domesticated animal, but I can manage that.'

'While you do I'll have a bath, I think.' She hesitated, then smiled almost shyly. 'And thank you—not just for helping, but for being here.'

Alec shook his head dismissively. 'I don't need your thanks, Cassie—now get a move on. When you've had your bath, get into bed and I'll bring your tea. Take advantage of the offer; it's not one I make very often.'

Cassie lay with eyes closed, up to her chin in steaming water, wondering how she'd cope once she was on her own again. Tonight, with Alec here, she felt safe. Tomorrow night could be a lot different. Suddenly she felt blazingly angry at the intruders. She felt soiled, as though the fingerprints they'd been careful not to leave downstairs were all over her body and mind instead. Combe Cottage had been her very own private place. She got to her feet abruptly, and turned the shower on her hair. Thoughts like that would get her nowhere. Nothing was changed. She could claim on insurance, get a new word processor, replace most of the other things in time, and just get on with her life. She was lucky. She could have been here when they'd broken in. She might have been mugged, or worse.

Cassie put on a scarlet cotton nightshirt from her suitcase, dried her hair as best she could with a towel in the absence of her stolen hairdrier, then climbed into bed a minute or two before Alec knocked on the door.

'Your tea, madam,' he called.

Cassie told him to come in and gave him a bright smile as he handed her a steaming mug. She sniffed suspiciously. 'You've put something in it!'

'Merely a squeeze of lemon from your fruitbowl, a teaspoon or so of single malt and some brown sugar.' He sat down on the edge of the bed. 'A little medicinal toddy to help you sleep, Cassie.'

'I do hope so.' She sighed as she sipped her drink, relaxing as the warmth spread through her veins. She slid a little lower in the bed as they talked for a while, discussing repairs to the kitchen door, which of all Cassie's possessions she needed to replace first. Alec leaned on one elbow against the brass footrail, his very presence calming Cassie's lacerated nerves as he strongly advised calling in a security firm as a means of avoiding similar episodes in the future. He finished his Scotch, then got up to take Cassie's empty cup and stood looking down at her questioningly.

'Think you can sleep now, Cassie?'

Cassie's teeth bit into her bottom lip. She hated the thought of being alone upstairs, even with Alec in the room below. She breathed in shakily, then gave him a diffident little smile. 'Alec, you don't have to sleep downstairs tonight.'

His eyes lit with a heat she could almost feel. He sat down on the bed and took her in his arms in one swift, purposeful movement, his mouth meeting hers with a possessive emphasis worlds away from a mere goodnight kiss. Cassie struggled a little, but it was a half-hearted, token resistance and Alec knew it. He held her still, his kiss deepening to a triumphant dominance she might have resented at any other time. But tonight she was all vulnerability, and in seconds all the fear and anger of the past few hours was transformed into sudden, overwhelming sexual response. Her whole body came alive, the blood rushing along her veins as Alec went on kissing her, taking her breath away, caressing her with hands at once gentle and relentless as he sought her response with a skill which rapidly brought them both to full, urgent arousal.

Cassie could feel his heart hammering against hers, the mutual heat of their bodies so intense that all she felt was relief when he stripped the scarlet cotton over her head. For a moment he hung over her, gazing down in triumph into her heavy-eyed, flushed face before his eyes dropped to her taut breasts and the temptation of erect, pointing nipples. Dark colour surged along his cheekbones and he breathed in deeply, then lowered his head until his dark hair brushed her breast and she gasped and arched her back in response to the caress of his teeth and lips and long, expert fingers.

At last Cassie let him know without words that she could endure no more of the exquisite torment and Alec leapt up to strip off his clothes. He reached to switch out the light and slid into bed beside her, pulling the quilt over them both to enclose them in a hot, private world where there was nothing but whispered endearments and heat and joyful, feverish, caressing hands and lips, and the explosive simultaneous gasp as their bodies were reunited at last, merging together instinctively in a rhythm so rapturously familiar, it could have been the thousandth time they'd made love together instead of only the second time in their lives.

A long, long time later, when the world was on its axis again, Cassie gave a stifled chuckle, her lips against the pulse throbbing at the base of Alec's throat.

'What's so funny?' he said gruffly, hooking a foot around her ankle to draw her closer.

Cassie slid a hand up to stroke his cheek. 'I just thought I'd point out that I meant you to sleep in the bed in the spare room—not mine.'

CHAPTER EIGHT

NEXT morning Cassie woke to find herself alone, and blinked sleepily, wondering if she'd dreamed the entire magical episode of the night. But certain protesting muscles, coupled with an unusual feeling of well-being, convinced her it had all been wonderfully, thrillingly real, a conviction reinforced by the smell of coffee floating up the stairs as she made for the bathroom.

A few minutes later she went downstairs in jeans and jersey, suddenly shy and awkward as a schoolgirl as she saw Alec at the breakfast table with the *Herald* propped against the coffee-pot. He sprang up at the sight of her, scotching her shyness by taking her in his arms and kissing her at such length that her cheeks matched her poppy-red sweater by the time he released her.

He grinned at her, looking tired but oddly younger, despite a day's growth of black stubble. 'Good morning, Cassie. How do you feel?'

'Dazed,' she said truthfully. 'Yesterday was a bit hectic, one way and another. How do *you* feel?'

Alec's lips twitched. 'Emotionally I'm on top of the world, but physically I'm fading fast with malnutrition. I skipped dinner last night in my hurry to see you.'

Cassie stared at him in horror, then rushed to the refrigerator. 'Then sit down before you expire, for heaven's sake. Fletcher fast-food service coming up!'

Blessing her mother for the box of basic necessities, Cassie soon had bacon and tomatoes grilling while she fried a couple of eggs. She set the food in front of Alec, put several slices of bread to toast under the grill and returned to the table with them to nibble at a slice herself while Alec demolished his plateful at top speed.

'Now,' said Alec, as she pushed the marmalade towards him. 'To work. How about house insurance? Do you have a claim form?'

Cassie jumped up, looking smug. 'Of course I do— filed neatly away in the appropriate place.' She went off to fetch the form and filled it in there and then so that she could catch the midday post.

'Right,' said Alec. 'I'll contact a security firm. In the meantime would you know a builder likely to do something about your door quickly?'

'I'll contact Mr Bowyer at the village stores. His finger's very firm on the pulse in Combe Aston—he's bound to know someone.'

'Good thinking. Once you've spoken to him, make a list of things you really can't do without and we'll go out and buy them.'

Cassie looked at him in surprise. 'Surely you can't want to go shopping for the kind of stuff I need?'

'Why not?'

'I—I don't know.' She flushed. 'Not your sort of thing, I'd have thought.'

Alec smiled wryly. 'It's not, as a rule. But as it's you, Cassie, I'll make the supreme sacrifice and help you choose whatever gadgets you feel you can't do without.'

'Top of the list is a kettle,' she said promptly, getting up to put another pan of water on to boil. 'And next a transistor radio. I feel cut off from the world without one.'

A phone call to the village shop soon provided Cassie with the number of a small local builder. Bill Turvey promised to see to her door that very evening, if she could wait until he'd had his tea.

'The Bowyers were surprised to hear from me,' said Cassie, as she sat down to a second pot of coffee. 'They thought I was still in Wales.'

Alec frowned as she filled his cup. 'You told them you were going away?'

'Of course. They deliver my newspapers. I cancelled them in advance when I was in the shop one day.'

'And while you were at it you had a little chat with them about visiting your mother?'

'I suppose I did—why?'

'Were there many people in the shop at the time?'

Cassie thought for a moment. 'Well, yes. It was quite full, I think. A few strangers as well as locals, which isn't unusual. We get a lot of visitors round here—especially when the weather's fine. The Bowyers display local crafts and pottery; quite a draw to tourists.'

'Then any number of people could have known you were away.'

Cassie bit her lip as she met the disapproval in Alec's eyes. 'Do you mean someone could have over-heard and decided to break in while I was in Wales?'

'It sounds very likely to me.'

'But no one in Combe Aston would do that!'

'It could have been one of these strangers you men-tioned. Or one of the locals could have let it drop quite innocently into the wrong ear.' Alec shook his head at her. 'Your profession probably makes you something of a talking point in the village, Cassie.'

She sighed. 'Maybe you're right. But my theory is the publicity angle. If anyone did drool over my pho-tograph in the *Herald* they were obviously turned on by my worldly goods, not my bodily charms.'

Having arranged with a security firm to call next day, Alec went upstairs to use Ben's razor just as the morning mail dropped through the door, followed by a peremptory knock. Cassie went to open the door, expecting the postman, her eyes widening for a va-riety of reasons at the sight of Liam Riley instead.

'Cassie!' He brushed past her into the sitting-room without waiting for her invitation. 'Are you all right? I heard about your break-in when I got in this morn-ing.' His eyes were darting in all directions, taking in the blank walls and lack of ornaments.

'I'm fine,' she assured him, giving a nervous glance up the stairs as she followed him into the room.

'Thank God you weren't here when it happened,' he said harshly, and swung round to face her.

'Amen to that! Nice of you to come, Liam.'

'Is there anything I can do?'

'I'm pretty well-organised, thanks. A builder's coming round this evening to mend the kitchen door where the burglar got in.' She took him into the kitchen to show him, then smiled rather awkwardly. 'How are the twins, Liam?'

His mouth twisted. 'They miss you. So do I. Look, Cassie—' He stopped short, his face suddenly wooden as Alec strolled into the kitchen, rolling down his shirt-sleeves.

The two tall, dark men eyed each other for a moment, then Alec held out his hand. 'Good morning. I'm Alec Neville.'

Liam shook the hand briefly, and nodded. 'Liam Riley—CID. I heard about Cassie's break-in.'

'Won't you have some coffee, Liam?' asked Cassie, praying he wouldn't say yes. She needn't have worried. Liam took in the breakfast table set for two, glanced from Alec's impassive face to Cassie's flushed cheeks and shook his head.

'No, thanks. Can't stop; my sergeant's in the car.' He nodded curtly to Alec then went with Cassie to the door. 'If there's anything I can do, any time, Cassie, just say the word.'

'Thank you,' she answered quietly, avoiding the

searching blue look trained on her face. 'Give Kitty and Tess a big hug from me.'

'Cassie,' he said in a rapid undertone, 'is this chap Neville the reason why you turned me down?'

'He's the old friend I told you about,' she said elliptically. 'The one I knew years ago when I worked at Pennington General.'

'Ah, yes. The new consultant plastic surgeon, no less.' His mouth twisted. 'I never stood a chance, did I?'

'That's nothing to do with Alec, Liam.'

'You mean I never stood a chance anyway,' he said bitterly. 'Thanks a lot. Goodbye, Cassie.'

Her dark eyes were bright with compassion as she held out her hand. 'Goodbye, Liam. Thanks for coming.'

He took the hand in a bruising grip, then dropped it and strode off down the path to the waiting car.

'So that's your inspector,' commented Alec when she went back to the kitchen. 'A trifle put out at finding me here, wouldn't you say?'

'I think it was the breakfast table that upset him.'

'Why?'

She coloured as she began to clear away. 'It's not a meal Liam's ever shared with me.'

'I hope you made it clear he's never likely to, either,' said Alec forcibly.

'Only I don't think we're talking about breakfast, are we?'

'No, we're not.' Alec suddenly pulled her into his

arms in a rib-cracking embrace, his face bent close to hers. 'I warn you, Cassie, I won't share you with anyone.'

She pulled away, feeling a sudden chill. 'Last night doesn't have to commit us to anything, Alec.'

His face drained of expression, his eyes suddenly cold as an Arctic sea. 'What, exactly, do you mean by that?'

'Just what I said. I'd hate you to feel, well, *obligated* because we slept together, that's all.' Cassie thrust dishes into the sink with unsteady hands, her back to the man eyeing her with ominous calm.

'But we didn't just *sleep* together, Cassie,' Alec said bitingly. 'We made love. More than once. And don't tell me it wasn't exactly the same magical experience for you as it was for me, because I refuse to believe it.' He strode across the kitchen floor and spun her round to face him. 'Are you telling me last night was just an urge for comfort on your behalf? If so I'd rather have given you a hot-water bottle and kept to the sofa as planned.'

Cassie scowled at him. 'I'm not trying to say any such thing.'

'Then what are you saying?' He dropped his hands suddenly and turned away, prowling round the room like a restless tiger. 'You've called the tune recently and I've let you do it because I accepted the fact that you wouldn't let me walk back into your life and automatically take up where we left off. But playtime's over, Cassie. I want sole rights where you're concerned—or none.'

'Are we back to ultimatums again, Alec?' she said hotly. 'I don't like them any more than you do!'

He turned round to face her, his eyes searching her face. 'Then the answer's no?'

'Alec, I'm not even sure what the question is!'

He frowned impatiently. 'Then I must be losing my touch. All right. First, I want you with me in Beaufort Square—'

'Give up Combe Cottage?' she interrupted, dismayed.

Alec's eyes narrowed ominously. 'Why not?'

'But I love it so much!' She waved a hand about her in a sweeping gesture. 'It's my very own special place. It would be like deserting a friend to leave here.'

'In which case it's a pity it's somewhat less of a bastion of security than it might be,' he snapped.

Cassie gave him a pleading look. 'Alec, couldn't we just go on as we are?'

'And how are we, exactly?' he enquired suavely. 'Tell me what you have in mind. Am I to come round on Saturday nights for dinner and a session in bed, while you come to me on Sunday for more of the same? Week nights are out, of course, because you're much too tired when you're working. But it's only fair to warn you that my own job might interfere just slightly with the programme, too. If someone's rushed into the General on a weekend needing fingers sewn back on I can hardly refuse my services because it's the only time Cassie Fletcher allows me something of her company.'

She stared at him, astonished. 'I can see you're furious, Alec, but I don't know exactly why.'

He clenched his teeth, the lines at the corners of his mouth suddenly deeply incised. 'No. You really don't, do you? Think about it when I'm gone, Cassie. It might dawn on you in time. When it does, let me know.'

Stunned at how quickly everything had gone wrong between them, Cassie stared incredulously as Alec shrugged himself into his jacket and strode out of the house without even saying goodbye, every line of him so taut with anger that it was all too reminiscent of the other occasion when he'd turned his back on her and taken himself out of her life.

She ran to the window, unable to believe he wouldn't turn back, but he drove off without a backward glance. Infuriated to find herself in tears, Cassie mopped herself up savagely, and pulled herself together. She had too much to do to let herself wallow in anguish over any man. First she rang the office equipment firm she used to order a new word processor, then she took her underwear and sheets from the washing machine and hung them out to dry in her pretty back garden. Afterwards she spring-cleaned every inch of the cottage, scrubbing floors and paintwork, cleaning windows, pushing the vacuum cleaner over every inch of carpet and giving herself no time to think until she was satisfied that no trace of her intruder could possibly linger anywhere. Then she locked the cottage and got in the car and made for Pennington and the shops.

As soon as Cassie got back, laden with kettle, radio, toaster and more groceries, Ben rang from work to ask how she was, and if there was anything he could do.

'You're the electronics genius,' she told him. 'Come and put plugs on my new purchases. I'll feed you as a reward.'

Cassie was perfectly capable of putting plugs on herself, but, much as she hated to admit it, she wanted company. It was Alec's company she wanted most, but, failing that, Ben's would do very nicely.

Ben arrived at the same time as Bill Turvey, the builder, for which Cassie was very grateful, since Ben chatted to the friendly man as he worked, leaving Cassie free to make a bechamel sauce to pour over fillets of mixed white fish and prawns and hard-boiled eggs. She topped the mixture with pureed potato, grated cheese over it and put the pie in the oven, then went to consult with Ben and the builder over the merits of a new door.

It seemed the intruder had tried to force the lock from outside before resorting to a hole in the glass to get at it from the inside. Bill Turvey pointed out splintered wood and eyed the remaining glass panel, expressing his disapproval of glass in an outer door.

Wouldn't Miss Fletcher fancy a nice new solid door, or, to be more precise, a nice old door?

'Got one or two hanging about. Often pick up a nice old fireplace or a door or two when some old house is demolished,' he told her.

Cassie thought it a splendid idea, and so did Ben. In no time Bill Turvey had taken measurements, nailed up a temporary piece of wood over the gap in the door, tidied up after himself and promised to return next day with a couple of doors for Miss Fletcher to see.

Cassie ran upstairs to wash and tidy herself up, leaving Ben to fix plugs to her new acquisitions. When she was in the bathroom she heard a knock at the front door and a murmur of voices as Ben answered it, and her heart soared. Alec! She ran downstairs and into the kitchen, then came to a halt, her disappointment overwhelming when she saw Liam Riley.

'Hello, Cassie,' he said warily. 'I just called in again to ask if you'd done anything about making this place more secure, lights and burglar-proof locks and so on. I know a reliable firm I could put you on to— old mate of mine started it when he retired from the force.'

On the point of telling him it was all in hand, Cassie changed her mind. Two estimates were better than one. 'Thank you. If you give me the number I'll ring tomorrow.'

'I'll ring him for you,' said Liam quickly. 'I'll put in a word, tell him it's urgent.'

Ben looked up from the last plug, grinning. 'Nothing like having the law on your side, Cassie.'

'Absolutely. Have a drink, Liam.'

He looked at the table, already set for two. 'I don't want to hold you up if you're expecting company.'

'My company's already here,' Cassie assured him, and waved him to a kitchen chair. 'Sit there and I'll get you a beer. It's more cheerful out here than in the other room—the bare walls in there get on my nerves.'

Liam, obviously glad to stay, sat down with a sigh, looking tired, and asked if the break-in had made Cassie nervous. He brightened when Ben assured him Cassie wouldn't be frightened by things that went bump in the night, because he intended occupying his sister's spare bedroom until Combe Cottage was made more secure.

'First I've heard of it,' said Cassie, surprised.

'No trouble,' Ben assured her airily. 'I can just as easily drive into work from here as from the flat for a day or two.'

It took very little persuasion to make Liam stay to share their meal. Cassie told Ben to open a bottle of wine as she set another place, then coloured a little when Ben whistled on finding a bottle of vintage Bollinger Alec had left on one of his recent visits.

'I assume you mean the plonk, not this?' he said, eyebrows raised.

'You assume right,' she assured him, and helped Liam to a large serving of fish pie.

Having expected a miserable evening after the quarrel with Alec, Cassie felt grateful for the company of her guests. They were halfway through the meal, laughing over Liam's description of his daughters' latest escapade, when a knock on the front door brought her to her feet.

When she opened the door Cassie went cold with dismay at the sight of Alec, standing stiff and erect like a guardsman, with a large flat parcel under his arm.

'Hello, Cassie. I thought I'd bring you a peace offering.' His brows flew together at the sound of masculine laughter from the kitchen as he eyed the napkin Cassie was still clutching. 'I'm sorry, I should have phoned first. I've obviously come at a bad time.'

Cassie found her voice with difficulty. 'We—we were just in the middle of dinner. Won't you join us? There's more than enough to spare, even with Ben on hand.'

'Taking my name in vain?' asked her brother cheerfully as he came to investigate. 'Hello there, we meet again, Alec. Why are you keeping him on the doorstep, Cassie?'

'I only came to deliver these,' said Alec quickly.

'What are they?' Cassie asked, secretly cursing fate for being so malicious. If Liam hadn't turned up it could have been Alec enjoying a meal with them. Now it was awkward for everyone, and Alec, being

Alec, wouldn't take kindly to seeing Liam with his feet under the table following hard on this morning's discussion.

'I thought you might find your bare walls depressing,' said Alec, his expression making it clear that he deeply regretted his charitable impulse. 'I saw these in the gallery off Beaufort Square.'

Cassie took the parcel reluctantly, and began taking the wrappings off two exquisite water-colours. Colour flew to her face, then drained away so drastically that the pictures shook in her hands as she saw they were studies of two woodland views, seen from opposite banks of a very familiar stretch of river.

Ben peered down over her shoulder in admiration. 'I say, I like those! Isn't that the River Penn?'

'Yes,' said Alec shortly. 'If you don't care for them, Cassie, you can exchange them for something else.'

'They're very beautiful,' she said unevenly, and forced her head up to look at him. 'How—how very kind of you.'

Alec returned the look in silence for a moment, then turned away. 'I'd better go.'

'You can't go yet!' said Ben, eyeing Cassie in disapproval. 'Come and have a drink with us—or some dinner. Cassie's made a fantastic fish pie thing. Liam Riley's sharing it with us, Cassie's friend from the force. Come and meet him.'

'I met him this morning,' said Alec, something in

his voice informing Ben that it wasn't a subject to pursue.

'Oh—right. Another time, then,' said Ben hastily. 'If you'll excuse me I'll just go back for seconds.'

Alec moved outside on to the garden path and turned to look at Cassie. 'It seems I should have been more specific.'

'About what?'

'Sharing.'

Her eyes flashed with resentment. 'This is my house, Alec. I choose who comes here, whether it's for a meal, or anything else.'

His lips thinned into a straight line. 'Your privilege, of course. But I'm surprised at the good inspector. He must be remarkably malleable to come chasing back the minute you crook your little finger.'

'He merely called in this evening to give me the name of a security firm he knows. Ben and I were about to have dinner, so we asked him to join us. End of story.' Cassie's chin lifted. 'Thank you for the water-colours. But they're far too valuable for me to accept as a gift.'

'Then throw the bloody things away,' said Alec savagely. 'What is it with you, Cassie? You won't take my gift, you prefer your precious cottage to the thought of marrying me—'

'Marrying you!' She stared at him, thunderstruck. 'Am I missing something? When did you ask me to marry you, for heaven's sake?'

'This morning—'

'You did not!'

'What the hell did you *think* I was talking about?'

'You said something about moving to your place—'

'At which point you threw up your hands in horror at the mere thought of vacating your little ivory tower here so I never got any further.' Alec's fists clenched at his side. 'This is degrading. I take exception to arguing on your doorstep.'

'It's you who won't come inside!'

'I'm bloody sure I wouldn't be conducting this conversation in front of an audience, least of all with Riley as part of it.' Alec controlled himself with visible effort. 'This is getting us nowhere. You misled me utterly and completely last night, Cassie.'

Her eyes narrowed ominously. 'And just how did I do that?'

'By convincing me I was the only man in your world.' His mouth twisted as a burst of laughter came from inside the house. 'Perhaps it's a feeling common to every man who shares your bed.'

'*What*?' she demanded, outraged.

'I'm not fool enough to believe you achieved such sexual virtuosity without a great deal of practice, Cassie,' he said unforgivably.

At which point Cassie slammed the door in Alec's face to prevent herself from blacking one of his furious blue eyes. She went back to her ruined dinner and put on the greatest act of her life right up to the moment she closed her front door again, this time after sending Liam Riley on his way.

Ben eyed her uneasily as she stared at the watercolours he'd laid carefully on the sofa.

'Shall I hang them up for you, Cass?'

She shook her head. 'No, thanks. They're going back to the donor.'

He blew out his cheeks. 'You've been like a volcano about to erupt ever since Alec Neville left. You two had a fight?'

'I suppose you could say that.' She smiled up at her brother's concerned young face. 'Lines of communication between Alec and me seem to have suffered terminal damage.'

'Can't it be put right?'

'I don't think so.' She shrugged wearily. 'I suppose I've got too used to pleasing myself lately. I'm not so clever at pleasing other people, apparently.'

'Did I do the damage by saying Liam was here?'

'No. I did. By asking Liam here in the first place.'

'But you didn't. He just dropped in.'

'Alec flatly refused to believe that.'

'Oh, I see.' Ben grinned. 'He may be mature and sophisticated, but your brilliant consultant's just as capable of base human jealousy as the rest of us lesser beings.'

'Apparently so.' Cassie gave an angry little laugh. 'I wouldn't mind, but I haven't given him any cause. I resent being made to pay the penny for a bun I never had the least desire for.'

CHAPTER NINE

ONCE she'd calmed down, Cassie decided against sending the water-colours back, certain the gesture would injure her relationship with Alec beyond all hope of repair. Added to that, she felt fiercely possessive about them. Ben had recognised the River Penn easily enough, unaware that the paintings showed the very stretches she and Alec used to walk along all those years before. The woodland alongside it had been their special, enchanted place, and just to look at the subtle, skilled studies brought all the sweet agony of first love flooding back so strongly that she couldn't bear to part with them. In the end she hung them together on the wall least exposed to daylight, where she could gaze at them to her heart's content from her favourite corner of the sofa.

Cassie's new word processor arrived in due course, but she found it hard to get to grips with her story again. The misunderstanding with Alec was more to blame than the break-in, and for a day or two Cassie answered every ring of the telephone at breakneck speed, certain he'd call. But he never did. The representative from the security firm came to see her, and at any other time Cassie might have been amused that the same firm had been contacted by both Alec and

Liam on her behalf. The double request had at least convinced the firm of the matter's urgency, and work began on the house only days later.

Soon Cassie had a solid, handsome new kitchen door, courtesy of Bill Turvey, also a burglar alarm, safety locks on every door and window, and, although nothing would persuade Cassie to have the original windows taken out and replaced by modern ones, she eventually consented to secondary double glazing which left her existing windows undisturbed. Long before the work was completed she sent Ben back to his own place, assuring him she would be perfectly happy on her own. Which was a long way from the truth. Cassie no longer felt nervous, but she missed Alec so much that she sometimes felt she'd never be happy again. Just being without him was a well-remembered pain, familiar from the last time. But, she reminded herself, she'd recovered from it before. In time she'd do it again. Which sensible conclusion did very little for her frame of mind, or for her sleepless nights. She wrote Alec a polite little note, thanking him for the water-colours, and added that Combe Cottage would shortly be as burglarproof as any house could ever hope to be. When no reply was forthcoming she finally gave up all hope of seeing Alec again and steeled herself to life without him.

By the end of a fortnight Combe Cottage was at peace again, leaving Cassie free to concentrate on her book. At which point she discovered a glaringly ob-vious mistake in her intricate plot and resigned herself to a lot of hard thinking to rectify it before she could hope to sit down at her word processor. Knowing of old the best method of stimulating her thinking processes, Cassie stripped the sitting-room and went into Pennington to buy paint. A burst of decorating would not only solve her plotting problem but at the same time rid Combe Cottage of any last traces of the break-in.

Attired in her gardening dungarees, T-shirt and sneakers, with her hair bundled up under a floppy old cricket hat of Ben's, and the radio turned up at full volume for company, Cassie perched on top of a ladder, wielding a roller with energy as she applied a second coat of white emulsion to the ceiling, taking care to avoid the beam which supported it. Absorbed in working out how to place the murderer in one location at the exact time a sighting of him had been reported somewhere else, she finished the last section with a sigh of relief for her aching neck, then almost fell off the ladder as a break in the music was followed by loud hammering on her front door. By some miracle she retained her balance and kept the ladder steady, acquiring a few white splashes on her face from the roller in the process before she climbed down and went to the door.

'Who is it?' she demanded irritably.

'Alec.'

Cassie swallowed hard, gave a despairing look at her paint-stained dungarees, then unhooked the new chain, shot the new bolt and opened the door.

Alec, in cords and roll-neck sweater, gazed at her with a poker-faced look she interpreted correctly as a strong desire to roar with laughter.

'Hello, Cassie. I met Ben in town. He said you might be in.'

'Why, Alec, *what* a surprise! I thought you'd never bring yourself to darken my doorstep again.' She smiled brightly, secretly furious with him for catching her in such a mess. 'A pity you didn't just ring up,' she added. 'As you can see, I'm rather busy.'

'Then I'll go,' he said, stiffening.

'No!' said Cassie involuntarily, only the paint on her hands preventing her from a grab at his cashmere sleeve to detain him. 'I mean, now you're here, you may as well come in.'

Alec unbent slightly. 'Thank you. Ben didn't say you were decorating, Cassie.'

'He doesn't know.' She pulled off the hat, shaking her hair free as she led him through the uncurtained chaos of the sitting-room straight through to the kitchen. 'It was a sudden impulse. I'm suffering from a bad attack of writer's block and to cure it started on some manual labour. It usually does the trick.' She finished scrubbing her hands and filled the kettle. 'Time for a coffee?'

'Yes. Thank you.' He leaned against the counter, watching her. 'Though really I should be doing much the same as you. Or had you forgotten I moved house last Monday?'

'No, I hadn't forgotten.' Cassie poured boiling water on instant coffee and handed him a mug.

Alec eyed her through the steam. 'You were going to help me move in.'

'I didn't dream you'd still desire my assistance,' she retorted, her eyes hostile as they met his. 'Is that why you came today?'

'No, of course it's not.' His jaw tightened. 'And I didn't ring first because I bloody well knew you'd hang up on me. Our last encounter wasn't exactly cordial.'

'True.' Her eyes glittered coldly. 'I take exception to orders, Alec, about my visitors or anything else.'

'I admit it was a mistake on my part. Not,' he added with sudden emphasis, 'that I feel much different on the subject.'

'I see.'

'No, Cassie, I don't think you do. Yet.' He straightened, his eyes holding hers. 'When I came across those water-colours I could hardly believe my eyes. I'd gone for a walk to cool off when I left you that morning. On my way back to the hotel I looked in the Beaufort Gallery, and there they were, the haunts of our youth just as I remembered them. I came round with them as an olive-branch and—' He shrugged. 'You know what happened next. I found Liam Riley where I wanted to be. It was like a punch in the stomach. Then to cap it all you slammed your door in my face.'

'So why *have* you come, Alec?' she asked quietly.

'A bundle of mail was redirected to me today from the Chesterton. Your note was among it.'

'It's quite a time since I wrote that,' she said, turning away.

'I know. I should have been in touch long before this. I was on the point of it several times. But hell, Cassie, apologies don't come easy to me—'

'In other words, you needed to hear from me before you'd make a move yourself!' she snapped.

'Yes,' he said morosely. 'Though in the end I'd have had to come. I miss you like hell.'

They stared at each other in silence.

'So what now?' said Cassie at last.

'Are you back with your inspector?' he said, as though the words were torn from him.

She breathed in deeply. 'Liam is a friend. One can't go ''back'' to where one's never been. But if I fancy offering him a drink or a meal when he spares the time to help me with my research, then believe me, Alec, I will.'

Their eyes met and clashed for a long, tense moment, then Alec nodded. 'Fair enough. I suppose I can live with that.'

'Who's asking you to?' she flashed back. 'I'm just making it clear that I lead my life the way I choose. I'm not twenty any more, Alec.'

'You look it, dressed like that.' Suddenly his face lit up with the rare, illuminating smile that never failed to demolish her defences. 'If anything, Cassie

Fletcher, you look a lot less.' He held out his hand. 'So now I've grovelled—'

'*Grovelled*?' Cassie let out an unwilling laugh. 'Is that what you've been doing?'

'It's as near to it as I get,' he assured her, and held out his hand. 'So shall we shake on it?'

Cassie put her hand in his, eyeing him doubtfully. 'On what?'

'Cessation of hostilities.' His grip tightened on her fingers. 'Leave the painting, Cassie. Come and have dinner with me.'

She pulled her hand away. 'No, Alec. I'm determined to start on these walls today.'

'Do them tomorrow,' he said inexorably.

Cassie pretended to think it over. 'Oh, very well,' she said at last. 'But you'll have to wait while I scrub the paint off.'

'Hurry up, then.' He gave her a little push towards the stairs.

'Wait—I've got to wash the roller and put the steps away— '

Alec took the roller from her and pointed to the door. 'Go. Provided you don't expect me to make a habit of it, *I'll* see to it.'

Half an hour later they were in the car on the way to Pennington, Cassie feeling infinitely more pleased with life than of late.

'So where are we eating, then?' she asked.

'At my place.' He glanced sideways at her. 'I thought you'd like to see it now the furniture's in.'

'I would, very much. Am I expected to cook?'

'No. I raided the local delicatessen.'

'Brilliant,' said Cassie, with a sudden yawn.

'Bored already?' he asked drily.

'I'm a bit tired,' she said with dignity. 'I've been working hard today. But I promise not to fall asleep over dinner.'

'If you do I'll just carry you up to bed.'

Neither seemed able to break the silence which followed this remark until Alec parked the car under the chestnut trees in the square.

'I merely meant I'd tuck you up in the spare room,' he said austerely, as he unlocked his handsome front door.

'Of course.' Cassie sailed past him, head in the air, then stopped short with an exclamation of pleasure.

The hall had gone unnoticed on her previous visit. Then it had just been an uncarpeted means of reaching the other rooms. Now it commanded attention in its own right, with a console table topped by a mirror in a gilded frame on the wall above it, and in a great bronze pot a weeping fig stood taller than Cassie between the gleaming mahogany doors leading to the downstairs reception-rooms. The whole of the ground floor was carpeted in the muted honey shade she'd helped Alec choose, she noted, pleased. In the waiting-room the walls were the colour of expensive milk chocolate as a foil to heavy unbleached linen curtains which hung to the floor from mahogany poles. Leather chairs and comfortable sofas were placed in groups, and as focal point a beautiful walnut drum table stood in the centre of the room, with neat piles of magazines and a centrepiece of dried flowers in a Chinese porcelain bowl.

'Exactly right,' said Cassie, impressed. 'If I were waiting here to be unstitched I probably wouldn't be scared at all.'

Alec looked amused as he led her up a graceful curve of stairs to his living quarters. 'Let's hope my patients feel the same. I'm afraid up here it's less grand. I did my splashing out downstairs to impress the punters.'

Cassie took to Alec's private sitting-room at first glance. A large Persian carpet, thin and fringed and even worn in places, added charm to a room with a rather crowded air of comfort. A pair of wing chairs were upholstered in worn leather, another pair in striped linen to match the sofa, and the curtains draped slightly on the floor as if the measurements had gone wrong. The fireplace had a leather club fender and a mantelshelf with pewter mugs and a French enamel clock, there were shelves with books and tables with lamps, a television and video recorder, an impressive stack of stereo equipment.

Cassie gazed around in silence, then turned to Alec. 'Was this your wife's taste?'

Alec shook his head. 'When she died I sold our flat furnished, lock, stock and barrel. These are the things I bought for the house in Roehampton. Though I suppose I should do something about the curtains—they don't hang properly.'

'I rather like them like that.' Cassie followed Alec to the kitchen, where a table was laid for two under a window which looked down on the garden. The kitchen was functional, but very pleasant, with white walls and pine cupboards and furniture, a black and white chequered tile floor, a set of copper pans hanging from a shelf.

'Those look very professional,' she commented, smiling, but Alec shook his head.

'Props. When I cook—which isn't often—I use French cast iron stuff. Just sit there and relax,' he added, as he took dishes from the refrigerator.

'Thanks. For once I'm thankful just to watch.' Cassie smiled. 'Besides, something tells me that Alec Neville in the role of chef is a pretty rare phenomenon.'

Alec put a crusty loaf on a wooden board and handed Cassie a breadknife. 'I've never pretended to be domesticated—you can slice some of that while you watch—but I'm not helpless. I can cook a simple meal if pushed, but I won't pretend I wouldn't prefer someone else to do it for me.' He raised an eyebrow as he removed the cork from a bottle of wine. 'I suppose I should have risen to the best china, and candles and so on in the dining-room.'

'I much prefer this,' Cassie assured him, and let him help her to slices of spiced ham and a wedge of game pie, a spoonful of chef's salad. 'So, if you don't like cooking, who's going to feed you now you've moved in here?'

'As a temporary measure, one of the women who come in to clean will provide an evening meal two or three times a week.' He shrugged. 'Otherwise I'll just eat out or make do with this kind of thing. Can I tempt you to a little more of anything?'

When Cassie shook her head regretfully Alec jumped to his feet and held out his hand.

'Before we start on the coffee, come and see the top floor.' He led the way to the trio of rooms upstairs, first to his bedroom, which was austere and uncluttered with a king-size bed and dark, severe furniture. The guest room's single occupant was a large brass bed, and a third room Cassie couldn't remember from her first visit was completely empty.

'This is the room I should be painting,' he told her.

'Is it to be a third bedroom?' asked Cassie.

'I'm not sure yet.' Alec led the way downstairs to the kitchen where coffee was bubbling in a complicated machine. 'So what do you think of my stab at interior decorating?'

'Couldn't have done better myself!' she assured him, then tasted the dark, fragrant liquid in her cup. 'Mmm, wonderful. You may not be much of a cook, Alec, but you can certainly make coffee.'

They lingered a little in the bright, pleasant kitchen, but after a while Alec suggested they move to the sitting-room and relax with some music. Cassie made for the comfortable striped sofa, and at Alec's suggestion slid off her shoes and swung her feet up with a sigh of pleasure, leaning back against a cushion with a smile of approval as she recognised the sophisticated, clever piano music of George Shearing.

'I like that,' she commented, yawning a little. 'Sorry. Nothing to do with boredom, I promise.'

Alec sat at the other end of the sofa, moving her bare feet over a little. 'From a purely professional point of view, Cassie Fletcher, I'd say it was the result of too many late nights. Those shadows under your eyes didn't come out of a box.'

Cassie met his eyes squarely. 'Not late nights, Alec. Sleepless ones.'

He held her gaze. 'Hang-ups from the break-in, or problems with the book?'

'All of those. But they're not the only reasons.' Suddenly she sat up, scowling. 'If you must know, Alec Neville, you're the reason I haven't been sleeping well.'

His face stilled. 'Why?'

'What do you mean—why?' She slumped back down again, turning away. 'You were pretty bloody to me the morning—'

'The morning I asked you to marry me,' he broke in swiftly.

Cassie's eyes flew to his, glittering with indignation. 'You did not! You never said a word about marriage.'

Alec smoothed a hand over her toes, tracing her pink-painted nails with his forefinger. 'We've been through all that. I vote we forget that morning—and the evening which followed it.' He looked up with sudden impatience. 'It's time to stop all this nonsense, Cassie. You know damn well we were always meant for each other. It's your fault we've spent ten years of our lives apart as it is. You're a woman now, not a girl of twenty. Surely you must be ready to settle down.'

As a proposal, whatever Alec was proposing, Cassie felt it left something to be desired.

'But I am settled,' she pointed out heatedly. 'I earn my own living, I own my own home—'

'You can't want to spend the rest of your life alone in that doll's house, Cassie!'

'Why not?'

'Because you were made for marriage and partnership—children too, if we're lucky, you obstinate little mule!' Alec's hand tightened in a bruising grip on her ankle as his eyes locked with hers. 'We're good together, Cassie. From the moment we met we always have been and you damn well know it. Nothing's changed. The minute I saw you across my desk that day I knew you were still the one woman in the world I'd ever really wanted.' He leaned forward until his eyes were blazing down into hers. 'I kept away until now to see if I could do without you, but I can't. Now look me in the eye and try to tell me you don't feel the same.'

Cassie stared at him defiantly. 'You don't mind,'

she said at last, 'that, according to you, I've been so sexually active during the interim?'

Alec's brows met in a fierce black line. 'I was angry, Cassie. I had no right to say that.'

Cassie put the flat of her hand against his shoulder and tried to push him away. 'How very true!'

'Forget I ever said it.' He caught the hand and held it against his chest, letting her feel the strong rapid beat of his heart against her palm. 'Give me one good reason why we should spend the rest of our lives apart. For God's sake let's get married, Cassie.' Suddenly he dropped her hand and moved to the end of the sofa. 'Or does this reluctance of yours mean you don't care for me?'

She shook her head vigorously. 'No, of course it doesn't. I won't pretend I spent all those years withering on the vine, Alec, but one look at you was enough to know I'd never stopped caring for one moment. But marriage would mean giving up certain things I've grown rather used to.'

'Apart from the cottage, name me one important thing marriage to me would deprive you of, Cassie Fletcher,' he demanded.

She smiled wryly. 'My independence for a start. You were always overpowering, Alec. Maturity has only reinforced that.'

'Rubbish!' he said forcibly. 'I wouldn't ask you to give up your writing—hell, I'm proud of your talent, Cassie.'

She sighed. 'But at the moment, Alec, I write

whenever I want. I try to keep to a routine, but the fact remains that the way my life is now I can work on in an evening or all day on a weekend if I want. That would have to change, wouldn't it?'

Alec shrugged. 'Would that be so impossible? It's not so much a change as a readjustment on your part.' He looked away. 'And if you were here with me I could stop worrying myself into a coronary wondering about your safety out there in the wilds.'

Cassie's eyes lit up. 'Do you really worry, Alec?'

'Of course I do,' he said savagely and pulled her into his arms, kissing her in a way which told her very plainly he was losing his patience fast. When he raised his head a fraction he smiled triumphantly. 'Why do you think I left that room empty up there? It's for you to decorate any way you want as your study.'

Her eyes lit with a mischievous gleam. 'Oh, well— why didn't you say that before?' She kissed him to let him know she was teasing, then pulled away a little, rubbing her cheek against his. 'I'll be very, very happy to marry you, Alec—no wait, please! You'll just have to give me time to get used to the idea.'

He hugged her close to him. 'Can't you ever just say a plain yes, Cassie Fletcher? All right, I'll give you time. Two weeks. How's that?'

CHAPTER TEN

No MATTER how much Alec argued, Cassie wouldn't hear of a date as early as that. She was determined to finish her book first and take time to enjoy planning a proper church wedding, with a small celebration afterwards, so that their nearest and dearest could be on hand to wish them joy.

'At least you can move in with me until then,' he said, eyeing her chaotic sitting-room with distaste when he took her home that night.

Cassie steered him through to the kitchen, and pushed him down in a chair. 'Alec, please, *please* don't be angry, but I'd rather not do that until we're married.'

He pulled her down on his knee and looked deep into her pleading eyes, his hands thrust in her hair holding her still. 'Why?'

Cassie slid her arms round his neck, and he relaxed a little, dropping his hands to her waist as she leaned her cheek against his. 'Until you came back into my life I honestly believed marriage wasn't for me. Ever.' She drew away, her eyes pleading. 'For just a very short time, until we're together forever and ever, can you understand that I'd like to stay here in my cottage for a while, enjoying all the anticipation and taking leave of the cottage and my old life at my own speed? I promise I'll never spend any more time away from you again, ever, if I can possibly help it.'

Alec's eyes softened as he brushed a hand over her untidy hair. 'When you look at me like that, how can I refuse you anything?' He kissed her gently, then with increasing heat, until suddenly he stiffened and drew away in suspicion. 'There's something else, too, isn't there?'

Cassie eyed him warily. 'Alec, would you think me totally strange if I said I'd like to wait until we're married before—well, before we're lovers again, too?' She waited, taut with apprehension, then to her relief the corners of Alec's mouth twitched.

'Not strange,' he said, resigned. 'Cruel, old-fashioned, possibly even a bit romantic, but, my darling Cassie, if that's what it takes to convince you it's not just your body I'm after, then abstention it is.' He traced a fingertip over her bottom lip. 'You were always different from any other woman I've ever known, Cassie Fletcher, which, of course, is why I love you. So I'll agree to your terms—as long as you don't keep me waiting too long. I could do without these cold showers I've been driven to lately.' He frowned, eyeing her stunned face questioningly. 'Now what have I said?'

'You said you loved me,' she said faintly.

Alec shook his head impatiently. 'Of course I love you! I was so much in love with you all those years ago it's a wonder I didn't do lasting damage to some of the patients at the General. I'm older now, lord knows, but no wiser where you're concerned. I'm still as mad about you as ever—jealous as hell of any man who looks sideways at you.' He shook her slightly. 'Not that you've ever professed similar feelings for me. Do you love me, Cassie?'

She ran the tip of her tongue round suddenly dry lips, and looked away. 'Why do you think I never married? After you it was out of the question with anyone else.' She gave him an oblique, melting look. 'Oh, Alec, you must know I love you.'

With a smothered exclamation Alec pulled her close and kissed her all over her flushed face, pressing kisses on her closed eyes and along her cheekbones and down her nose until he reached her mouth, and kissed her there with such hunger that she was ready to forget about waiting another second, let alone until their wedding night. But suddenly he pushed her away and jumped to his feet.

'Enough of that, Cassie Fletcher,' he said, breathing hard, 'or I'll do something you'll regret.'

Cassie's change of heart was written so plainly on her flushed face that Alec clenched his teeth and shook his head.

'No, Cassie. I've said I'll wait, so I'll wait. It may kill me,' he added menacingly, 'but never let it be said that Alec Neville went back on his word!'

Cassie soon found she'd discovered the cure for writer's block, and it was nothing to do with decorating. After spending most of the next day with Alec, making plans and telephoning her mother and Ben, she was so eager to get back to her book that she was furious with herself for starting on the sitting-room. Very early on the Monday morning she set to with a will, wielding paintbrush and roller to such effect that the room was soon spick and span and Cassie back at her desk, all the threads of her plot unravelled and re-woven into a complex story that she was confident was her best so far.

Time seemed to fly by, in spite of Alec's constant grumbles that their spring wedding-day was too much in the future for his preference. He bought Cassie an exquisite Victorian sapphire ring, Kate and Mike came up for a weekend to meet him, the church was booked and, because Combe Cottage was too small and Bryn Morfa too remote, a caterer was hired to serve a wedding breakfast in the house in Beaufort Square. Cassie lived in a state of happiness so intense that she sometimes forgot to eat as she finished working on the final chapters of her book.

'Tonight,' she said to Alec when he arrived at the cottage a couple of weeks before Christmas, 'the dinner's on me. I've finished—I sent the manuscript off to my editor today! Let's go out and paint the town red.'

Alec laughed as Cassie took a bottle of Bollinger from the refrigerator. 'At last! I wondered when you'd find an occasion worthy of it.'

'You produced the champagne when you gave me

this,' she reminded him, turning her ring lovingly on her finger. She raised her glass, smiling radiantly. 'To Quinn Fletcher, bless her little cotton socks.'

It was an enchanted evening. They dined at the Blue Boar, a local inn noted for its imaginative food, but their absorption in each other's company was so complete that they hardly noticed what they ate. Afterwards Alec drove the short distance to Combe Aston at a leisurely rate, and followed Cassie into the cottage with a possessive air about him which half amused and half thrilled her to bits. Once locked in privacy inside, she went into his outstretched arms with a sigh of delight which intensified to a gasp as they closed about her in an iron embrace. He began kissing her with a hungry dominance which seemed part of the celebration, whispering gratifying, inflaming things in her receptive ear as he sat down on the sofa with her and laid her back against the cushions, his lips tracing a path over her closed, dreaming eyes, and down her face, then parting hers with a fierce hunger as she locked her arms around his neck. His hands moved to the place where her silk shirt impeded his caresses, then he dropped his face to the hollow between her breasts and grasped her waist with hands which bruised.

Alec raised a taut, urgent face to hers. 'Cassie, I want you so much I'm going crazy. I'll wait until we're married if it kills me, but why did you set the date so far away?'

Cassie looked at him with dazed, heavy eyes. 'We—we don't have to keep to it.'

Alec tensed. 'What do you mean?'

'There's nothing to stop us bringing the date forward—if we want,' she added, her eyes suddenly bright with excitement. 'You can alter the hotel booking in the Seychelles and if the caterers can't manage it I'll get someone else—I'm sure the vicar will alter the date. You could even get a special licence...' She trailed away at the astonishment on Alec's face. 'Or is that a bit over the top?'

'Can this be the Cassie Fletcher I know and love?' he queried huskily, then gathered her into his arms. 'Your enthusiasm's balm to my soul, my angel. Do you mean it?'

'Every word,' she assured him. 'As you once pointed out, Alec Neville, life isn't a dress rehearsal. So let's get on with the show!'

After a frantic interval of rearrangement and phone calls and hasty shopping on the part of the bride and the bride's mother, Catherine Quinn Fletcher was married to Alexander Murray Neville on New Year's Day in the small Norman church of St Mary in the village of Combe Aston, with Alec's brother and family from Scotland in attendance, a psychologist friend of Alec's from his Cambridge days as best man, and various friends and colleagues of both bride and groom to toast the happy pair afterwards at the hastily rearranged reception at the house in Beaufort Square.

'Though I'd love to know why you suddenly changed your mind about the date, Cassie,' said Kate afterwards in private, before going off to Combe Cottage for the night.

'It suddenly seemed so pointless to wait,' said Cassie happily. She eyed her reflection in the mirror in the bedroom she would share with Alec that night. A radiant creature in an ivory wool dress smiled back at her, eyes glittering like stars in a flushed, happy face beneath hair which had consented to stay up in the knot the hairdresser had entwined with small white silk flowers. 'It isn't as if we're teenagers, Mother.'

'If anything,' said Kate drily, 'you look rather younger than you did as a teenager, Cassie. And very, very pleased I am to see it. Be happy, darling, and have a lovely time in the Seychelles. Bring Alec down to us as soon as you can when you get back.'

Mr and Mrs Alec Neville were spending their wedding night in Beaufort Square before flying off next day in search of sun and relaxation for three weeks' honeymoon as a prelude to their life together. The cottage was up for sale, and to Cassie's surprise she felt quite philosophical at the thought of someone else in possession of Combe Cottage. Now she was married it seemed like a finished chapter in her life.

Alec was amazed to learn this later when they were alone at last, close together on the sofa, a tray of champagne and titbits beside them as they talked over the day.

'I'd have thought you'd hate the very idea of some- one else in possession of your beloved cottage,' he said lazily, smoothing a hand over her loosened hair. Both of them had changed out of their wedding finery, Cassie into her new cream satin nightgown and crim- son velvet robe, Alec into one of the tracksuits he used for jogging round the park in his more energetic moments.

'So did I,' she confessed, and looked up at him with a smile. 'Perhaps I've learnt to count my bless- ings.'

Alec rubbed his cheek against hers possessively. 'Do I take it you number me as one of them?'

'Top of the list,' she assured him. 'How many peo- ple get a second chance? Oh, Alec, I'm so lucky— even if it did take me a while to recognise it.'

'The good luck is mine, angel,' he contradicted, and lifted her on to his lap. 'We've travelled a long way to get to this point in time, Cassie. I can hardly believe we're together at last.'

'Then I'll try to convince you,' she whispered, and raised her mouth to his, locking her hands behind his head as he returned the kiss with a tenderness which changed very quickly to an urgency he made no at- tempt to control. Cassie responded with such unin- hibited ardour that Alec tipped her off his lap, jumped to his feet and swept her up into his arms.

'No more waiting,' he said with sudden force, and started for the stairs.

Cassie burrowed her head against his shoulder. 'Amen to that!'

He laughed unsteadily, breathing heavily by the time he reached the bedroom. He deposited her on the bed without ceremony, stopping only to throw off the tracksuit before kneeling beside her to untie the silk girdle of her robe. Careless of its splendour, he tossed the crimson velvet on the floor, then stretched himself out beside her, caressing her through the satin before he stripped it over her head and began to kiss her with mounting need, his invading tongue receiving an eager welcome as his hands roved in caresses which inflamed every part of her into quivering, impassioned response. Cassie moaned, helpless to control her arching body as his skilled, relentless fingers brought her to the very edge of ecstasy before he surrendered to the urging of his own senses and united their bodies at last in mutual pleasure so intense it was almost pain as they achieved the ultimate in physical harmony.

Cassie dozed, exhausted, in Alec's arms for a while, only to rouse a little later to his questing hands and the touch of his lips as they woke her to eager, warm response. It was the early hours of the morning before, still clasped tightly in each other's arms, they finally slid into deep, dreamless sleep.

The first fingers of grey light were showing through a crack in the curtains when Cassie woke, disorientated, to the brush of close-cut black curls on her bare shoulder, a warm arm so heavy across her stomach it hurt. She shifted a little, gently removing the arm, then breathed in sharply, as she realised the weight of Alec's arm had nothing to do with her discomfort. Her back was aching, so was her stomach. She ground her teeth in dismay. Her system, never of the most reliable variety, was about to prove very inconvenient—and embarrassing. Don't be silly, she scolded herself silently. Alec's a doctor. He knows all about women and their little vagaries. Only this was no ordinary vagary, she discovered in alarm. The ache in her back grew suddenly unbearable, as the cramps in her stomach worsened to a gripping, frightening pain.

Cassie inched her way across the bed, desperate to get to the bathroom, but as she sat up the wrenching pain took her breath away and she gave a gasping little moan.

Alec shot up, instantly awake. 'Darling, what is it?'

'I feel a bit off,' she said inaccurately, and tried to smile over her shoulder. 'A bit embarrassing really. The usual female thing, Doctor—.' She caught her breath, biting back a groan.

Alec leapt out of bed and pulled on his dressing-gown as he raced round to her side of the bed. Cassie hunched over with arms locked across her stomach, sweat pouring down her face.

'Give me your hand,' Alec ordered and glanced at his watch as he felt her pulse, but she shot up with sudden urgency, oblivious of her nakedness as she brushed past him to shut herself in the bathroom. Alec gave her a few moments' grace then opened the door without ceremony, pulled her to her feet and swathed her in a bath-towel. Cassie clutched at him convulsively as another spasm of pain gripped her, and he held her tightly until it passed, then carried her back to the bed and laid her down gently.

'Is it always as bad as this?' he asked in concern. 'I'll go and make you some tea—'

'No! Don't leave me,' implored Cassie wildly, then stared up at him in horror as another spasm convulsed her body, only this time she barely had time to draw breath before it returned again, and then again and again, and Alec made no further move to leave her, other than to pack towels beneath her before staying with her to do everything necessary as the slim body writhed in agony on the bed where only hours before it had joined with his in such heart-stopping rapture.

Later that evening Cassie lay like an effigy in a bed in a pretty room at St John's Nursing Home, her body a little more comfortable but her mind still in agony. She'd seen Alec briefly after coming back from Theatre, but he'd said little other than to smooth her tangled hair and tell her he'd be back later to visit. She lay staring at the window, unable to come to terms with the miscarriage. How could she have been such a fool? she thought dully. Her system was an irregular mechanism which often suffered a hiccup, so the usual signs had failed to register. She'd lost weight, felt less enthusiasm for food lately, but had put any irregularity down to her rush to finish the book, the shock of the burglary, all the other recent excitement in her life—anything other than pregnancy.

A compassionate, soothing nun brought her some tea and Cassie drank it gratefully, but when coaxed to eat shook her head. All she wanted was Alec.

But when he arrived later, looking pale and drawn, Alec was not the comfort she'd hoped for.

'How are you feeling?' he asked, and read the chart at the end of her bed before pulling a chair near to sit down.

No kiss, thought Cassie numbly. She would have liked a kiss. Not much to ask of a bridegroom.

'I think the term's "as well as can be expected",' she said wearily.

'I rang Combe Cottage but your mother and Mike had obviously left for Wales. I'll ring them there later and tell them what happened.' Alec eyed her questioningly. 'Shall I ask Kate to come back?'

'No!' A tear slid from the corner of Cassie's eyes and Alec handed her a tissue. 'Unless,' she added thickly, 'I'll be a nuisance—interfere with your work.'

'I'm not supposed to be working,' he reminded her. 'You won't be a nuisance, Cassie. In a few days you'll be yourself again.'

'That's all right, then,' she said, sniffing, and eyed him unhappily. 'I'm sorry about the honeymoon, Alec.'

He gave her a twisted smile. 'Short, wasn't it?'

Cassie clenched her hands under the covers. 'I meant the Seychelles.'

'The least of our worries.' He got up and took her hand. 'You need sleep, Cassie. Time I was off.'

The tears welled up again. 'But I wanted to *talk*!'

'Not tonight,' he said firmly. 'Time enough when you come home. I'll fetch you in the morning.'

Cassie looked at him for a long moment, then turned her head away. Alec, she knew perfectly well, was concealing anger behind that controlled exterior. But she was in no state to cope with it. Explanations would have to wait.

'What message shall I give Kate?' he asked.

She breathed in shakily, keeping her eyes averted. 'Give her my love. Tell her as soon as I'm—I'm fit, I'll drive down to see her.'

'Very well. Get some rest now. I'll be back in the morning.' Alec hesitated, then bent to kiss her cheek fleetingly, Cassie convinced the caress was solely for the benefit of the nurse who came in to see if Mrs Neville required anything.

After a night spent agonising over Alec's coldness Cassie was appalled by the sight which confronted her in the bathroom mirror next morning. Her ashen face and dark-ringed eyes weren't much like a blushing bride, she thought bitterly.

With a different nun in attendance she went through the tiring process of bathing, dressing in the clothes Alec had brought, but by the time she'd brushed her hair into submission and tied it back she felt exhausted, in no mood for the breakfast brought to her.

Sister Joseph coaxed and cajoled, and to please her Cassie drank a little orange juice, but refused anything else other than tea. She drank the entire contents of the pot on the tray, as she sat in an armchair with the morning paper to await Alec's arrival.

When he finally came, looking in little better shape than Cassie, he had Charles Conway with him, the gynaecologist who'd been a guest at their wedding barely a day before he'd given up a game of squash to perform the small operation necessary after Cassie's miscarriage. He, it seemed, was obliged to pronounce her fit to leave before Alec could take her home.

Deeply embarrassed, Cassie submitted to his ministrations while Alec waited outside, and an hour later she was back in Beaufort Square, installed on one of the sofas in the sitting-room with a coffee-tray in front of her while Alec stood in front of the fireplace, looking down at her with cold, questioning eyes.

'Why didn't you tell me, Cassie?' he said without preliminary.

Cassie sighed with relief, eager to get the explanations over so that they could get on with their honeymoon, wherever they spent it.

'I honestly didn't know,' she told him, as she handed him his cup.

Alec put it down on the mantelshelf with a bang

which threatened to break it. 'Didn't know! Do you think I'm a fool, Cassie? You must have known.'

She shook her head and took a reviving sip of coffee. 'I've always been plagued by a very irregular system, Alec. When nothing happened for a couple of months it never occurred to me to suspect anything different.'

Alec sat down suddenly in one of the chairs. 'You're asking me to believe that?'

Cassie stared into his grim, pale face with sudden anger. 'Of course I am. It happens to be the truth.'

Alec raked a hand through his hair, eyeing her with a look of such bitterness that she quailed. 'For a writer who dreams up intricate plots, isn't that a bit feeble?'

'Alec—' she began, but he put up a long, slim hand to silence her.

'I had a long time to think last night, and eventually everything began to slot into place.'

Cassie stared at him blankly. 'What do you mean?'

'The way you suddenly had the brilliant idea about bringing the wedding forward. Before I, or anyone else, could suspect your reasons.' He shook his head as she started to protest. 'Let me finish. Suddenly you were all for getting married in a rush, and I, like a fool, believed you'd had a change of heart. And all the time you were carrying another man's child.'

Cassie's eyes widened in utter disbelief, her face suddenly like parchment as it lost what little colour it had. She clenched her teeth to keep them from chattering with shock, unable to say a word in her own defence, as Alec's bitter, rasping voice went on, stripping her of every illusion she'd possessed.

'Wasn't an inspector of police good enough for you, Cassie? Did it suddenly occur to you that with a child to interfere with your writing a successful consultant might be a better provider than a policeman already burdened with a family to support?' He leaned forward suddenly, until his accusing white face was only inches from her own. 'That's why you let me make love to you after the burglary at the cottage—as a safety measure so I'd think the child was mine.'

Cassie saw his face through a faint mist. Perspiration started up in the roots of her hair and on the palms of hands she clenched tightly, determined not to let Alec see how low his accusations had brought her.

'You're wrong,' she whispered.

'Oh, I don't think so, Cassie.' His smile sent a shiver down her spine. 'When I couldn't sleep last night I remembered I'd never read the book you signed for me after your talk. I took it to bed with me, in lieu of any other company, and frankly, Cassie, it was a revelation.'

Cassie stared at him mutely, breathing shallowly to control her nausea.

'I was expecting a routine whodunnit,' went on Alec, as though discussing some writer he'd never met. 'But *Mortal Sins* was pretty gory, with lots of pathology details and a particularly cruel cat-and-mouse-type murder. You write remarkably well, but the really riveting bit was the love interest between your Detective Sergeant Harriet Gale and the pathologist—Rufus something.' Alec's eyebrows rose. 'The love-scenes, Cassie, positively sizzled. No wonder your books sell. And last, but by no means least, from his description the object of the lady's passion is the spitting image of Liam Riley.' He breathed in deeply, his eyes glittering like ice. 'Well? Have you anything to say?'

Cassie looked at him with weary, unbelieving scorn. 'As it happens, I could say a lot. But I'm not going to demean myself with explanations you are obviously in no mood to believe. But I will say one thing, Alec Neville. You may be a brilliant surgeon, and far more clever than lesser mortals like me, but you're also quite extraordinarily *stupid*.' She struggled to her feet, then gasped as the room spun round her and she crumpled, unconscious, into arms which shot out to catch her.

CHAPTER ELEVEN

WHEN Cassie came to she was in bed. She struggled to sit upright, then slumped with her head on her raised knees, reliving the scene downstairs in painfully complete detail right up to the moment she'd given way to the faintness she'd been fighting ever since she got home.

Only this wasn't her home, she thought grimly. This was Alec's home and Alec's bed, and she wasn't going to stay in either a moment longer than she could possibly help. As if she hadn't enough to cope with, just lying here brought back memories of her wedding night, and she wasn't equipped to cope with those at the moment. Besides, sharing this bed with Alec would mean sharing the bathroom, which smacked too much of intimacy in the present circumstances. Cautiously she slid her feet to the floor, and made her way shakily to the spare room. To her relief the bed was made up. She slid between the cool, welcoming sheets and closed her eyes, trying to make her mind a blank.

Soon, when she was a bit more herself, she would work out what to do next. But for the moment it was too much effort even to care. But that, she knew of old, would pass. She'd had experience of Alec's insults before. His accusations of playing him false with another man had been no less unfounded when she was twenty than they were now, more than ten years later. But Alec still had more power to hurt her than anyone else in the world.

Cassie dozed for a moment or two, only to surface with reluctance to the sound of Alec's voice repeating her name as he grasped her hand in an ungentle grip.

'Cassie! What the hell are you doing in here?'

She opened her eyes on his grim, accusing face. 'I was trying to sleep,' she said stonily. 'Perhaps you'd be good enough to go away and let me do so.'

'You needn't have bothered. I intended sleeping here myself,' he bit back.

'I've saved you the trouble.' Cassie turned her head away wearily.

'You need to eat.'

'I don't want anything. Thank you,' she added politely. She felt the bed give as Alec sat down on it, retaining his grip on her hand.

'Cassie, I'm speaking as a doctor now, not—not your husband.'

She turned her head to smile scornfully into his bleak face. 'Goodness, Alec, how that stuck in your throat. Don't worry, I won't hold you to the title. We'll make other arrangements as soon as possible.'

Alec's eyes gleamed with cold arrogance. 'Certainly not. You can't divorce me—I've given you no cause. And I've no intention of divorcing *you*.'

She frowned. 'No? How strange! After all that diatribe downstairs I thought it would be your first priority.'

'Ah, but there are certain advantages in having you for a wife, Cassie,' he observed suavely, and smoothed a finger over the back of her hand. 'You're physically attractive, a talented writer, an interesting companion, even a good cook, and where bed is concerned your talents outstrip all the rest. Why would I want to div-orce you?'

Cassie stared at him, incensed, her dark eyes enormous in her pallid face. 'You gave me plenty of reasons not so long ago.' Her eyes narrowed. 'Or do you value public opinion? I suppose it would look bad if you gave me the push straight on top of the miscarriage and so on. Your reputation might suffer. People might even share your suspicions about the father of the child. Bad news for your ego.'

'You're the one who lacerates my ego,' he said savagely, and got up. 'Now pay attention. Unless you eat, Cassie, you'll find yourself back in hospital, so I'm going to heat some soup—and stand over you until you've swallowed some of it.' Alec halted at the door, looking down at her hostile face. 'By the way, I've had Ben on the phone, full of concern, needless to say, with instructions from his mother to report on your progress. I told him he could come round this evening.'

By the end of the week Cassie felt physically a lot better. Mentally she was, if anything, worse. Several times she'd decided to try her hand at convincing Alec how wrong he was about what had happened, but the truth sounded so lame, even to her own ears, that she balked at the effort. Ben visited her for a few minutes most days, bringing chocolates and books and a video she'd wanted to see. He was sympathetic and affectionate, but obviously so embarrassed about her miscarriage that Cassie vetoed all talk on the subject, as much for his sake as her own. She talked at length to Kate on the phone and promised to drive down to Wales as soon as she felt strong enough, and in the meantime lived in a kind of limbo with Alec, the relationship between them best described as a painful, uneasy truce.

Alec soon began seeing patients again at the house, and once Cassie was a little stronger he returned to his work at Pennington General and the Burns Unit. The holiday, as he was careful to refer to it, could be postponed until Cassie was better. His receptionist, Margaret, would field all calls, and would be only too happy to provide any help his wife required.

The first time Alec was away from the house for an entire day Cassie packed a bag, waited until Margaret was out at lunch and left her a note to say she'd be out all afternoon. She put some provisions in a bag, then rang for a taxi and asked the driver to take her to Combe Aston. When she arrived at the cottage Cassie turned the heating on high, stretched out on the sofa with a bestseller Ben had brought her and, for the first time since Alec had fired his hail of accusations at her, began to relax.

When the telephone rang at seven that evening, the time Alec was due home, Cassie lifted the receiver and said calmly, 'Hello, Alec.'

'How did you know it was me?' he demanded.

'My lovers have already been in touch,' she said with sarcasm.

There was silence for a moment.

'Cassie, you're not well enough to be on your own,' he said at last with some constraint.

'You're wrong there, Alec,' she contradicted gently. 'For the first time since my miscarriage I actually feel better.'

'Because you're back in your beloved cottage,' he said bitterly.

'You can't deny that it's been a strain lately, just being in each other's company,' she said reasonably. 'It's more relaxing here—with no one to remind me of my apocryphal sins.'

'Apocryphal?' he said sharply. 'It's the first time you've even hinted at any form of denial.'

'Alec, what on earth would have been the point? You played judge and jury, tried, convicted and sentenced me. I can't offer you a shred of proof to convince you that what you said was untrue. Why should I waste time and effort in trying?'

Another silence.

'Are you staying at the cottage permanently?' he

asked at last, as though the words burnt like acid on his tongue.

'No. Don't worry, I won't embarrass you by running away. If you like, you can come and fetch me later, then first thing in the morning you can send Margaret up to me with some kind of message, and no one will ever know I slipped the net for a while.'

'Cassie,' said Alec, so quietly that it sent a chill down her spine. 'I don't care a toss what Margaret thinks. If it makes you feel any better to stay at the cottage overnight, or even longer, then do so.'

'In that case, I will. Goodnight, Alec.' Cassie put the phone down without waiting for his response and settled herself to enjoy a peaceful evening on her own.

But to her dismay she soon found herself regretting her decision to stay. The wind was high and there were creaks and groans in the timbers of the cottage, and even with the television turned up high Cassie felt distinctly nervous. This was nonsense, she told herself crossly. She had never paid any attention to the noises before. It was simply because the cottage had been cold for a while and the central heating was creating all sorts of sound effects. She made herself an omelette for supper, but failed to enjoy it because in addition to the internal noises she began to imagine she could hear footsteps outside. This, she informed herself, was a side-effect of writing thrillers. Her imagination was transforming every perfectly ordinary noise into something sinister. Controlling an urge to ask Alec to come and get her, she went upstairs to switch on her electric blanket instead. She turned her radio up, put on her warmest winter nightgown and got into bed with her book after pushing an armchair under the handle of the door.

A good thing Alec couldn't see her, she thought, pulling a face. He probably thought she was luxuriating in her solitude. If she were honest she'd expected the same. Unfortunately, angry with Alec though she might be, and wounded to the heart by his lack of trust, she still loved him passionately and wanted to be with him far more than she wanted to be anywhere else. Her return to the cottage had been of some use, if only in teaching her that. Though nothing in the world would have made her admit it to him.

Cassie spent a miserable night, listening to the wind howling, afraid to put her light out and unable to sleep with it on. She fell into a heavy doze just before dawn, and awoke later, headachy and irritable, with the telephone shrilling in her ear.

'Cassie?' said Alec. 'Are you all right?'

'Yes,' she lied gruffly. 'Why wouldn't I be?'

'I didn't know whether you'd taken anything to eat.'

'Of course I did, Alec. I'm not entirely brainless.'

'No,' he said tonelessly. 'I never thought you were.' He paused. 'When had you thought of coming home?'

Home? Cassie looked around her at the bedroom.

She'd been so sure she'd always look on this as home. And now she wasn't sure at all. Not that the house in Beaufort Square was any more like home, either. But at least she wouldn't be alone there.

'Cassie?' said Alec. 'Did you hear what I said?'

'Yes, Alec. I'll drive back this morning. My car's still in the garage here.'

'Don't do that. I'll come for you.'

'There's no need—'

'I'm on my way to St John's right now,' he interrupted tersely. 'I'll be finished there about midday. I'll pick you up on my way to lunch.'

Cassie put the phone down with a sigh, then switched off the light and drew the curtains, feeling foolish as she removed the chair from the door. Her fears seemed silly by the light of day; nevertheless she'd been scared here on her own. Which made the idea of Combe Cottage as a retreat a bit impractical. Up to last night she'd been determined to withdraw it from the estate agent's list, but now she wasn't so sure. Cassie had a bath, rummaged in her wardrobe for some brown tweed trousers and her clover-pink sweater, found some thick brown wool socks and slid her feet into her flat suede shoes, then brushed her hair and tied it up with a brown velvet ribbon and went downstairs to make herself some breakfast.

While she was eating it the phone rang again. Cassie scowled. If Alec intended checking up on her every half-hour she'd go mad!

It was his receptionist, Margaret, who informed

Cassie that an Inspector Riley had rung, asking if he might see Mrs Neville.

'I wasn't sure what I should do,' she said anxiously, 'so I told him you were out and to ring back in half an hour. Mr Neville said you'll be back for lunch but this Inspector Riley seemed anxious to speak to you as soon as possible. Shall I give him the phone number at Combe Aston?'

Cassie thought for a moment. 'Actually, Margaret,' she said slowly, 'when he rings, tell Inspector Riley to call round here. He knows the address. If he can't, tell him I'll be in Beaufort Square this afternoon.'

Curious to know why Liam was anxious to see her, Cassie finished her breakfast and washed up, not at all surprised soon afterwards to hear a car drive up and Liam emerge from it to stride up the front path. Cassie watched him from the window in approval. There was a spring in his step, and he looked visibly younger.

She hurried to answer the door, welcoming him in with a bright smile.

'Hello, Liam. Come in. Have some coffee—or shouldn't you be wasting taxpayers' money on social calls?'

To her surprise Liam gave her a swift kiss on the cheek, then followed her into the kitchen, assuring her he'd be delighted to drink coffee with her. 'Because I'm not actually *on* a social visit,' he informed her.

'Oh, lor', it's a fair cop, guv,' said Cassie, holding up her hands.

Liam laughed, then sat down at the kitchen table, looking relaxed and very pleased with himself as he watched her fill a kettle and set out cups. 'This visit just happens to kill two birds with one stone,' he informed her. 'Even three,' he added, with a sheepish smile. 'First of all, Cassie, congratulations—on your marriage, I mean. Bad luck you were taken ill before you could go on your honeymoon.'

Cassie eyed him closely as she handed him a mug. 'Who told you about that?'

'Ben. I rang him up last night to ask for your phone number, and he said you'd been under the weather.'

Cassie sat down opposite him, and leaned her chin in her hands as she looked at him ruefully. 'It was a bit more than that, Liam. I had a miscarriage.'

'No!' He stared at her, appalled. 'Hell, Cassie, what can I say? Ben didn't go into details.'

'I'm not surprised.' Cassie drank some of her coffee. 'Anyway, let's not talk about that. You said you had three things; what are the other two?'

Liam looked as though he'd have liked to say more in the way of sympathy. Instead he patted her hand and went on to amaze her by saying that some of her possessions had been recovered.

'Liam, you're kidding!' she said in astonishment.

He assured her he wasn't. A series of car-boot sales in the Banbury area had proved a rich source of stolen goods. The thieves had been caught, and Cassie's Meissen figurines, her pictures and the Pembroke table were now in police custody.

'None of the electrical stuff yet, I'm afraid, but maybe they'll turn up in time, too,' added Liam.

'I don't care about those—it's Gran's figures and my mother's table I'm concerned about.' Cassie jumped to her feet and gave Liam a smacking kiss. 'How sweet of you to come in person to tell me. When do I get my things back?'

As soon as they arrived in Pennington, Liam informed her, then smiled in a way which had Cassie intrigued.

'Come on, then, Liam. What's the third thing?'

'Detta and I are back together,' he said sheepishly as he got up to go.

Cassie threw her arms round him impulsively. 'Oh, Liam, I'm so glad. For you and the girls. Kitty and Tess must be so happy.'

'They are indeed. But Cassie, what about you?' He touched a hand to her pale cheek. 'You look as though a gust of wind would blow you away. Was Neville very cut up when you lost the child?'

'That he was, Liam.' Cassie gave him a bleak little smile. 'Nothing will convince him it wasn't yours.'

When Alec came to collect her he examined Cassie with a professional eye and told her she did indeed look better.

'Is it the country air, or just the stay in your cottage?' he asked as he carried her overnight bag to the car.

'Probably a combination of both,' she said mendaciously, and gave him a very straight look as he got in beside her. 'Liam Riley came round to see me this morning.'

Alec's hands clenched on the wheel. 'Hasn't the man the decency to leave you alone now you're married, for—?' He clamped his mouth shut and switched on the ignition, gunning the engine slightly as he drove up the rough surface of the lane towards the main road.

'He rang Beaufort Square first,' said Cassie, ignoring the interruption. 'And his motive was not a spot of illicit congress with the new bride, believe it or not. He came to tell me some of my things have been recovered.'

Alec thawed slightly. 'Oh. I see. I'm sorry. Frankly, I thought you'd seen the last of that lot.'

'So did I.' Cassie glanced at him. 'He also came to tell me he's back with his wife and daughters, and very happy about it.'

Alec frowned. 'He told you he was happy? Bloody tactless, wasn't it, in the circumstances?'

'What circumstances?' she asked tartly. 'As far as Liam's concerned he's back where he belongs, and I'm very glad for him—and for Kitty and Tess.'

Alec drove in silence for a while, then, as though he couldn't keep the words back, he asked whether she'd told Liam about the miscarriage.

'Yes, Alec. I did.' Cassie stared straight ahead through the window, her face set.

'And how did he react?'

'He was appalled.'

'As well he might be,' said Alec violently, in a tone which killed any attempt at explanation on Cassie's part.

That evening they sat down together in the dining-room to eat a simple, well-cooked meal provided by Mrs Lucas who came in to clean. Cassie would have preferred it in the kitchen, but since Mrs Lucas had insisted on staying on to serve it they had no choice but to go through with the charade, complete with candles and wine which turned the entire meal into a farce.

Cassie pushed food around her plate, but ate very little of it, though she drank down two glasses of wine as if it were lemonade, with the result that after two cups of coffee later on she was rewarded with a dull headache and bade Alec goodnight before going early to bed.

This, she thought, while she was waiting for a couple of pain-killers to work, wasn't any way to live a married life. Tomorrow she would go to Wales. When Alec came in later to see if there was anything she wanted she gave him the news.

'You can't drive all that way. You're not well enough yet, Cassie,' he said flatly. He had no need to add that he forbade her even to think of it. The look on his face said it for him.

'I shall go by train,' said Cassie, and looked away. 'I—I would quite like to be with my mother at the moment, Alec.'

He sighed deeply. 'Naturally, Cassie. I can under-stand that. I'll drive down at the weekend to fetch you back.'

Cassie gave him a mutinous look. 'I may stay longer than that.'

'As you wish. But I'll drive down at the weekend to see you anyway.'

'Why?' she demanded, wincing at a spasm of pain in her head.

'Because I bloody well want to,' he said savagely, and strode from the room.

Kate was hard put to it to hide her concern when she picked Cassie up from the station in Carmarthen. 'You look terrible,' she said bluntly. She tucked a rug round Cassie's knees and got in beside her, eyeing her daughter's face with anxiety. 'I'm surprised Alec let you come.'

Cassie's eyes flashed. '"*Et tu, Brute*?"'

Kate bit her lip. 'Ah, I see. He's not happy about it.'

'About the journey, not the destination. I'm afraid he's coming down at the weekend to make sure I'm behaving myself. I hope you don't mind.'

'Your husband's welcome any time,' said Kate gently. 'It's only natural he's worried about you, Catherine.'

Cassie winced. Her mother rarely used her proper name. 'It's not quite as simple as that, Mother,' she said wearily, then smiled. 'I've come to you for advice. I hope you've got lots to give.'

With tact, Mike, who had given Cassie his usual affectionate welcome when she arrived at Bryn Morfa, took himself down to the local for an hour that evening after dinner to give Kate time alone with her daughter. Cassie told her mother the whole story, then sat back and waited, sure her mother would be ready to black Alec Neville's eye for even daring to doubt her precious daughter's story.

'But Cassie, as far as I can gather you haven't even tried to tell him the truth,' said Kate, after thinking it over.

'I shouldn't *need* to,' said Cassie passionately. 'He should have trusted me—' She ground her teeth in irritation as the phone interrupted them, then eyed her mother mutinously when Kate came in from the hall to say Alec wanted to talk to her.

'Couldn't you just have told him I'd arrived safely?'

'Cassie, go and talk to your husband. At once.'

Thirty years old she might be, but Cassie still jumped when her mother used a certain tone of voice.

'Hello, Alec,' she said dispiritedly.

'I'd hoped you'd ring as soon as you arrived,' he informed her, the rasping quality in his voice very much in evidence.

'I didn't know exactly where you'd be.'

'It's gone eight, Cassie; you know damn well where I am by now!'

'Sorry,' she muttered. 'I didn't think of it.'

'Your honesty's hellish unflattering!'

'Sorry. Anyway, Alec, I'm here in one piece and I'm fine. Well, not wonderful, but I'm perfectly all right.'

'Good. I'll be with you on Saturday in time for lunch—as Kate insisted just now, I hasten to add.'

'I'm sure she did. Fine. See you then.'

'Cassie, take care of yourself—please.'

'With my mother on hand I'll hardly fail to,' she assured him, something in his voice bringing a lump to her throat. 'Goodnight, Alec.'

Cassie spent the days until the weekend in the constant company of her mother, sometimes with Mike as well, though he took care to leave the two women together more than usual once he'd heard Cassie's story. And now she was away from him Cassie found her animosity towards Alec beginning to lessen. As Kate strongly advised, when he came on Saturday she would swallow her pride, tell him the simple truth about the pregnancy and perhaps here, on neutral ground, they might have a better chance of sorting things out than in Pennington. That Alec loved her she never had the slightest doubt. All she wanted— yearned for—was for him to trust her as well, and believe what she told him.

One complication in her life Cassie hadn't looked for was snow. When she woke up on Saturday morning the world was white. She shivered and threw on some warm clothes then went down to breakfast, finding Kate and Mike equally surprised by the weather.

'I thought it never snowed in these parts,' said Cassie accusingly.

'It doesn't often, so near the sea. Perhaps you should ring Alec and tell him not to come,' said Mike, after they'd listened to a weather forecast on the radio.

'I suppose so,' said Cassie carelessly, secretly shattered by disappointment at the thought. But when she dialled the Beaufort Square number the only answer was Alec's curt message on the answering machine. Alec, it seemed, had already left. Cassie reported to the others, accepted more coffee, discussed some of the news items with Mike, then after breakfast kept herself as busy as possible by helping Kate. By noon the house was immaculate, the table laid, a selection of vegetables prepared and mouthwatering smells were coming from the oven. But Cassie, fully expecting to feel weary, found she was still edgy and restless. She went upstairs to have a bath, choose some clothes, fiddle with her hair; tried some colour on her cheeks, then wiped it off again. She leaned on her hands on the windowsill and stared down the narrow road winding away through a still white world, reminding herself that if the newspapers and the milk had arrived without any hold-ups Alec would too. But the restless, anxious feeling refused to subside. The weather report at noon had been discouraging. Snow showers were expected in all parts, some of them heavy. Surely, she reassured herself, Alec would have enough sense to stop off somewhere if the weather got really bad.

Suddenly Cassie rummaged in her wardrobe for an old wool beret and long, striped scarf, found some sheepskin mittens and went downstairs to borrow Kate's heavy caped raincoat.

'I'll take Taff for a bit of a stroll,' she announced, stamping her feet into rubber boots. 'I won't be long.'

'Don't go too far,' warned Mike.

'And don't slip,' added Kate. 'Those gorgeous flannel trousers won't take kindly to a roll in the snow.'

Cassie laughed and whistled to Taff, who came running, bouncing up and down like a barking rubber ball in his joy at being let out into the wonderful white world outside. The steep drive was treacherous underfoot, but once they reached the narrow road itself the going was better, shielded so well by hedge-topped stone walls that the surface was free of snow in places. A car would have no problem. Always supposing it made it down the hairpin bends from the main road, of course. She put that thought from her with a shiver, and began hurrying after Taff, who wanted to go chasing off across the fields. In the end she was forced to clip on his leash, and he walked at heel amiably enough, looking up at her with something suspiciously like a laugh on his hairy, bright-eyed face as he trotted obediently by her side. Cassie marched along at a brisk pace, feeling better for the exercise, but after a while a snowflake landed on her nose, quickly joined by several more, and suddenly she was in the thick of one of the promised heavy snow showers and began to hurry back the way she'd come. Taff bounded along beside her, enjoying the whole thing enormously, but Cassie was in less than peak condition. By the time she reached the house and the two anxious people watching out for her, she was out of breath and only too glad to subside on a kitchen chair while Mike yanked off her boots.

'Has Alec rung?' she gasped as she pulled off the damp beret.

'No, darling. Perhaps he doesn't want to waste time looking for a call-box.'

'Mother, he's got a phone in the car!' Cassie jumped to her feet, hung the sodden raincoat on a hook behind the kitchen door, and looked at her watch, tight-lipped. 'He's late.'

Mike assured her it was hardly surprising, handed her a glass of sherry, patted her shoulder and told her to go and sit in front of the fire and stop pouting.

'Pouting!' said Cassie indignantly, then grinned reluctantly, and did as he said, the effort of joining in intelligent conversation for a few minutes helping just a little to stem the fear rising inside her in an insidious tide.

By two o'clock Kate insisted they drink some of the soup intended for the first course at lunch, and leave the rest of the food until the evening meal. By the time they'd cleared away afterwards no one was even pretending not to be anxious.

'Perhaps I'll just ring the AA and get a road report,' said Mike, only to return to the other two a moment later looking troubled. 'The line's dead,' he reported. 'No wonder Alec hasn't rung.'

'No! How will I know if he's had an accident?' said Cassie wildly, and went over to the window, clutching her arms across her chest as she stared out into the blizzard outside. 'He could be out there somewhere right now, lying in a ditch—or worse—'

'Stop that at once,' said Kate sharply, and seized Cassie's arm. 'Now just you come over to the fire and calm down.'

Cassie breathed in deeply, pulled herself together and smiled shakily in apology to Kate and Mike. 'Sorry. Let's play cards or backgammon or something—I need occupation!'

As she settled down to backgammon with Mike for a while Cassie felt better. The blizzard outside lessened, the room was comforting in the glow of the fire when Kate switched on a lamp or two as darkness threatened even earlier than usual. They had the radio for background as Kate knitted and Cassie and Mike wrangled amiably over the backgammon board, but it was a surface tranquillity. Lurking beneath her determined calm, fear was paralysing Cassie's brain to the point where she conceded defeat far more easily than usual, and, unable to sit quiet any longer, she sprang up to make some tea just as the lights went out and the radio went quiet, leaving only the crackling fire for light and warmth.

There was energetic activity for a while as Kate lit candles and Mike went outside to the garage for the camping stove and a cylinder of gas, accompanied by a barking Taff, who thought it was all some new game as Mike went back and fore to bring in a plentiful supply of logs for the fire. Cassie rummaged in a drawer for batteries for the radio, while Kate unearthed a heavy old iron kettle to put on the fire to boil water, grumbling that the power could have been kind enough to last a minute or two longer until they'd made their tea.

'At least the casserole's done,' said Cassie brightly, as she put cups on a tray. 'We can do the vegetables on the camping stove, and—and—' Suddenly her face crumpled and she threw herself into Kate's arms. 'Oh, Mother, where *is* he?'

Kate hugged her daughter close. 'Even knowing Alec as little as I do, I'm still perfectly sure he'll get here eventually. Just allow a little longer for weather conditions, that's all.'

Comforted by her mother's sane common sense, Cassie kissed Kate's cheek and went rushing to help Mike as he juggled with a pile of logs on his way through the kitchen door with the excited Taff. When the noise had abated slightly Mike's head lifted.

'Quiet, boy! I can hear something down in the lane.'

They all rushed to the door, peering through the gloom as the snow-muffled sound grew nearer, a vehicle of some kind, but slow-moving and noisy and nothing like the distinctive sound of Alec's Daimler. It halted at the bottom of the drive, and Cassie heard raised voices, listened for a moment then tore off down the drive, her feet slipping and sliding in her flat suede shoes as she made straight for the man who dropped his bag and threw out his arms to catch her as she slid the last foot or two into his cold, wet embrace.

'Where the devil have you *been*?' she screeched, and threw her arms round Alec's neck as he bent his head to kiss her, neither of them paying any attention to the snow still whirling around them.

'Where do you think I've been?' he rasped, raising his head for a second, then kissed her again, and kept on kissing her until Mike came with a barking, frisking Taff to interrupt with a suggestion that they continue with what they were doing indoors, preferably in front of the fire, before they both got pneumonia.

Once inside, with the greetings to Kate over and his leather jacket taken away for some tender loving care from his hostess, Alec stood in front of the fire with a mug of steaming coffee laced with brandy, Cassie held close in the crook of his free arm while he related his adventures.

'I called in at the Burns Unit before I came away this morning,' Alec began. 'By the time I got away the weather had deteriorated.' He looked down into Cassie's upraised face. 'But I was in a hurry to get here so I took off anyway. I hadn't gone far before I realised I should have gone the long way round and driven down a couple of motorways before I really got to grips with the Welsh countryside, but by that time I was committed.'

Driving in and out of heavy snow showers *en route*, Alec had made his way slowly along the picturesque route through mid-Wales, trying at intervals to ring Cassie to report on his progress, but without success.

'The telephone's not working,' Cassie informed him, smiling up at him with such warmth that Alec lost the thread of his story.

'Where was I?' he said huskily, blind to the indulgent looks Kate and Mike were exchanging.

'Somewhere in Wales,' said Cassie, moving closer.

Alec turned back to the others with an apologetic smile. 'For once this coast is getting the worst of the snow. The Cardigan road is passable, but the minor road down here was a nightmare. Those hairpin bends must be a challenge in normal weather, but today you need a kamikaze temperament to cope!'

Alec had sought directions at a farm after a perilously close call on one of the sharpest bends, praying he was at least somewhere in the vicinity of Bryn Morfa, and to his surprise and everlasting gratitude the farmer suggested Alec garage the Daimler in his barn and accept a lift on a tractor for the last mile or two.

'So here I am,' said Alec, and drained the contents of his mug. 'I'm cold, damp, late, and very, very glad to be here.'

'No happier than we are that you've arrived!' said

Kate with fervour, and got up. 'As you can see, it's not just the telephone we lack *pro tem*, so dinner may be slightly behind tonight. Fortunately the main course is cooked, but the rest of it will be a test of ingenuity on the part of Mike and myself.' She smiled at the tall man holding her daughter captive. 'Alec, this fire helps heat the water fortunately, so there's plenty of hot water for a bath. Have a good rest afterwards before you come down for a pre-dinner drink. There's plenty of time.'

'What a jewel of a mother-in-law,' said Alec, putting a couple of candlesticks on the dressing-table as Cassie closed her bedroom door behind them. 'Kate obviously realised I wanted you to myself for a while.'

Cassie smiled and went into his outstretched arms. 'Shall I run your bath?'

'Not yet.' Alec tipped her face up to his. 'Darling, could we just go to bed for a little while? Just lie there together and hold each other while I tell you how much I love you and what a swine I've been, and how I don't deserve to kiss even your little toe?'

'I don't want you to kiss my little toe. Not first of all, anyway,' she said, giggling, and stripped her scarlet jersey over her head. 'Come on, then, Alec Neville; last one into bed pays a forfeit.'

'What do you want?' panted Alec, who, after much cursing over a knotted shoelace, was a fraction behind her in getting under the covers.

Suddenly Cassie was very serious. They lay face

to face in each other's arms in the soft, flickering light, as Alec waited, tense, to hear what she had to say.

'Tell me what forfeit you want me to pay, Cassie,' he said at last, his voice tight with suppressed emotion.

'I want you to trust me. I know you love me,' she added quickly, 'but that isn't enough, Alec.'

He let out a deep, unsteady breath. 'You don't need to spell it out, Cassie. God forgive me, I said such bloody awful things to you it's a wonder you even let me through the door. It's a long time since I shed any tears, Cassie, but I was near it just then when you came hurtling into my arms out there.'

'I was worried,' she said tersely. She shuddered and wriggled closer. 'I kept thinking of you lying in a ditch or in hospital somewhere, and no one knowing where to get in touch with me.'

'So you still love me, Cassie,' he said, letting out a deep breath, and kissed her with a tenderness which for the moment had no relationship to desire. 'I don't know how you can.'

'Neither do I,' she said gruffly. 'You were a pig, Alec Neville.'

'I was out of my mind with jealousy, my darling!'

'That's an excuse?'

'No, an explanation.'

Cassie drew away a little, frowning suddenly as she stared up into the shadowed face close to hers. 'But I haven't explained anything yet, Alec.' Her eyes lit up with such sudden brilliance that Alec blinked and rubbed his cheek against hers. 'Does this mean you trust me without hearing *my* side of the story?'

He raised his head and looked at her with eyes dark with remorse. 'I'd give a lot to say yes, Cassie, but at this stage in our lives you deserve the complete, unvarnished truth.' He clenched his jaw for a moment, then breathed in deeply and went on, his eyes holding hers as he told her that Liam Riley had called round to see him the night before to return Cassie's belongings. 'He told me I was a bloody fool who didn't deserve a wonderful wife like you, that he'd have given his right arm to make love to you, but had never been granted the privilege. He made a few more pithy comments, very much to the point, then went home to his wife and daughters leaving me feeling like Napoleon after Waterloo.'

Cassie lay very still, her eyes wide with astonishment. 'Good heavens,' she said, awed. 'I wonder what made Liam do that?'

'Not what, Cassie, who!' Alec's mouth twisted. 'I wonder if Mrs Riley knows how close she came to losing her husband altogether? I got the distinct impression that if you'd crooked your little finger at any point the story would have been different.'

'No,' said Cassie decisively. 'You've forgotten Kitty and Tess. Detta had a greater hold over him than ever I had.'

Alec's stern face looked unconvinced. 'So now you

know it was Riley who put me straight, are you disillusioned?'

Cassie thought about it. 'Not as much as I expected. After all, if you didn't care, why did you insist on coming here this weekend before you ever saw Liam? You could have let me run off to Mother and just wait until I got back.'

'I couldn't do that,' he said huskily, and kissed her gently. 'The moment you got on that train I knew that whatever reason you had for marrying me I couldn't care a fig what it was, just as long as you had.' He looked deep into her eyes. 'I've known a lot of women in my life, Cassie. You know that. But the only commitment I've ever made, other than to you, was to Helen. I didn't enjoy finding her with her one-time lover, but my pride suffered more than my feelings, which were mainly guilt afterwards, coupled with a few more seeds of distrust to add to the ones you planted in my heart ten years ago.'

She reached up a hand to smooth the frown lines between his thick black brows. 'Is that why you leapt to the wrong conclusion about the baby, Alec?'

'I suppose it contributed.' His mouth twisted. 'It cut me to pieces, Cassie. It's hard to believe now I know the truth, but the thought of you pregnant with another man's child drove me mad. I behaved like an idiot, I admit, but you could have put a stop to it, darling!'

''How?' she demanded indignantly.

'All you had to do was tell me the truth at any point and I'd have believed you.'

'Would you, Alec?' she said with meaning. 'Would you, really?'

He closed his eyes and held her cruelly tight against him. 'I devoutly hope so, Cassie. You must know I love you, but the very fact that I love you so much means I'll always be jealous, even when you're old and fat and grey.'

She swallowed hard, and rubbed her cheek against his. 'Oh, Alec, what a lovely thing to say!'

He kissed her again, harder. 'So I'm forgiven?'

'Yes.' Cassie returned the kiss in a way which clarified her feelings so perfectly that her husband gave way to the feelings which had been threatening to get out of hand ever since they got into bed together.

'Cassie,' he said, after a while, a note in his voice which turned her bones to water. 'I had a bath this morning.'

'That's nice,' she said, giggling like a schoolgirl. 'So did I.'

'So since we're two such shiningly clean people, why waste time in the bathroom when we can just stay here until it's time for dinner?' said Alec, and ducked down beneath the bedclothes.

'What are you *doing*?'

'Kissing your little toe!'

Their shared laughter was the overture to a reunion of such tenderness and joy that Cassie knew she'd look back all her life on that candlelit room in snow-bound Wales as the setting for the true beginning of their married life.

'Do you realise, Alec Neville, that this is our second reunion in just a few short months?' said Cassie drowsily, as she watched Alec dress.

He nodded, smiling down at her flushed face in its frame of wild, unruly hair on the pillow. 'Second and last,' he said with emphasis, as his face emerged from the neck of his sweater. 'From now on we keep together as much as is humanly possible, madam.' He held out his hand. 'Up you come, sleepyhead. Kate and Mike are being enormously tactful, but we can't stay here any longer.'

Reluctantly Cassie left the warmth of the bed, and began pulling on clothes in feverish haste, absurdly embarrassed at having an audience for the process. 'Stop looking at me like that,' she scolded, as she dived into her jersey.

'Give me one good reason why I should!' He smiled at her, the hard blue eyes alight with an expression she knew, with a sudden leap of the heart, was reserved for her and her alone. 'Right. Now you're decent, come here for a moment.'

'You were the one who said we must go,' she reminded him, as their arms closed round each other.

'I just needed to say one more thing, my darling.' Alec raised her face to his with a gentle forefinger. 'I'm so deeply sorry about the baby. Not only for my bloody awful suspicions, but because we lost it. I talked to Charles before I came away. He says there's absolutely no reason why we shouldn't have more. As many as we want.'

'Oh, Alec,' she said unsteadily, and hugged him close as she smiled radiantly into his eyes. 'You can't know how happy I feel just to hear you say that.'

'From now on I promise to try to understand everything you feel,' he assured her, and kissed her lingeringly, then blew out the guttering candles and pulled her to the door in the darkness. 'At the moment I'd hazard a guess that you feel hungry. I hope so. I'm starving.'

They laughed together as they felt their way along the landing towards the muted glow below. Suddenly Cassie came to a halt at the top of the stairs.

'Just one more thing to clear up, Alec.'

'Keep it short, for pity's sake! I'm expiring from malnutrition.'

'Just for that I'm not sure I'll tell you.'

'Tell me what?'

'Why I called you stupid.'

Alec's attention was caught. 'Ah, yes,' he said grimly, his hands gripping her waist. 'I'd forgotten that. Keep talking.'

'Remember how furious you were about the love scenes in my book?'

'Only too well!'

'Think back to the description of Rufus Cairns. Tall, broad-shouldered, bright blue eyes and dark hair.'

Alec tensed. 'You said a "shock of dark hair", Cassie. Just like Riley's.'

'Wrong. Just like yours—the way it used to be ten years ago.'

Alec's fingers bruised her skin. 'Are you telling me *I'm* the model for this Cairns character?' He pulled her down suddenly, until they were sitting side by side on the top stair. 'And the love scenes?'

'If you read the book again you may find a certain familiarity about those too, Alec Neville,' she said tartly. 'Or have you forgotten what happened in the boat-house all those years ago? Everything I know about love I learned from you—' The rest of her words were lost against Alec's mouth as he lifted her on to his lap to go on kissing her with such absorption that neither noticed when the lights came on.

They parted suddenly, blinking, as a tactful cough from the hall below interrupted them. They sprang to their feet to see Kate smiling up at them with a deep glow of thankfulness in the brown eyes so like Cassie's.

'Now we can see to eat it, could you two possibly manage to consider something as mundane as food? Mike and I are famished.' Her smile widened mischievously. 'Just spare us twenty minutes or so at the dinner-table then we'll leave you in peace until breakfast!'

'It's your fault we're late,' hissed Cassie, laughing, as her mother disappeared in the direction of the kitchen.

'How do you make that out?' demanded Alec, pulling her by the hand as they hurried downstairs to join the others.

'It's that bedside manner of yours, Doctor—I couldn't resist it!'